FIRE PROPHET

OTHER BOOKS IN
THE SON OF ANGELS: JONAH STONE SERIES

Spirit Fighter

FIRE PROPHET

Son of Angels

JONAH STONE

Book 2

JEREL LAW

THOMAS NELSON

Since 1798

NASHVILLE   DALLAS   MEXICO CITY   RIO DE JANEIRO

Published in Nashville, Tennessee, by Tommy Nelson. Tommy Nelson is a registered trademark of Thomas Nelson, Inc.

Tommy Nelson® titles may be purchased in bulk for educational, business, fund-raising, or sales promotional use. For information, please e-mail SpecialMarkets@ThomasNelson.com.

Scripture quotations are from The King James Version of the Bible; The New King James Version. © 1982 by Thomas Nelson, Inc. Used by permission. All rights reserved; the Holy Bible, New International Version®, NIV®. © 1973, 1978, 1984, 2011 by Biblica, Inc.™ Used by permission of Zondervan. All rights reserved worldwide. www.zondervan. com; The Holy Bible, Today's New International Version®. © 2001, 2005 by Biblica®. Used by permission of Biblica®. All rights reserved worldwid,e. "TNIV" and "Today's New International Version" are trademarks registered in the United States Patent and Trademark Office by Biblica®. Use of either trademark requires the permission of Biblica.

Library of Congress Cataloging-in-Publication Data

Law, Jerel.
    Fire prophet / Jerel Law.
       p. cm. — (Son of angels ; bk. 2)
    Summary: When the powers of the Evil One threaten to destroy eighth-grader Jonah and the other humans who are one-quarter angel, Jonah is led by a series of visions to find the one person who is meant to call upon God's faithfulness and save them—a prophet of Elohim.
      ISBN 978-1-4003-1845-2 (pbk.)
     [1. Angels—Fiction. 2. Good and evil—Fiction. 3. Prophets—Fiction. 4. Christian life—Fiction.] I. Title.
PZ7.L418365Fi 2012
[Fic]—dc23   2012010659

Printed in the United States of America

12 13 14 15 16 17 QG 6 5 4 3 2 1

For Bailey,
who is beautiful,
both inside and out

CONTENTS

CONTENTS

PART I

QUARTERLINGS

(children of the nephilim, who are one-fourth angel)

What are mere mortals that you are mindful of them,

human beings that you care for them?

You made them a little lower than the angels;

you crowned them with glory and honor

and put everything under their feet.

Hebrews 2:6–8 TNIV

ONE

CHINATOWN

Jonah and Eliza walked down the street together, trailing their parents and their younger brother, Jeremiah, who was stopping to ask every street vendor he saw a question, not worrying that they were all old Chinese men and women who didn't speak English. Jonah, however, was looking for something much more sinister than kind old men and women selling vegetables and toys. He stopped to look at the wooden cart full of strange-looking vegetables, but continued to keep one eye on the crowd of people milling by.

He and Eliza had been practicing their newfound angelic powers every day they could, back in the woods behind their home in Peacefield, always careful to make sure no one was spying on them. After all that had happened last year, they figured they couldn't be too careful. But even though Jonah felt his skills getting sharper, he couldn't deny that he had been even more on edge recently.

"You've been paranoid all day," Eliza said. "Can't you just relax and have some fun?" She threw a ginger root at him playfully.

He brushed his dark hair out of his eyes and threw the ginger back at his sister.

"No!" shouted the glaring merchant behind the vegetable table. "Stop!"

Jonah felt his face flush as they hurried away from the table, continuing to cut his eyes back and forth across the street.

He'd felt like this ever since they'd stepped off the subway and set foot in New York this morning, like a shadow had fallen over him. Even though it had been almost a year since they'd been here last, it seemed like it was yesterday.

Last September, Jonah had discovered their mom was a nephilim, a child of a human and a fallen angel, which made him and his brother and sister one-quarter angel, or quarterlings. His mother had been kidnapped by Marduk, a fallen angel who was Abaddon's right-hand man, and Jonah and Eliza had raced to New York City to rescue her, with the help of their angel friends. They had discovered the world-behind-the-world known as the hidden realm, battled fallen angels, and finally faced Marduk himself. Jonah's mind flashed back to the battle, and how, with Elohim's help, they had defeated Marduk and the rest of the Fallen. In spite of their victory, there were days Jonah still couldn't believe he and Eliza had made it back, with their mom, alive.

"Maybe you don't remember what happened last time we were here as clearly as I do," Jonah said with a grimace. He and his sister had won a battle, but the war between Elohim's and Abaddon's forces was still raging, and he knew that they could be attacked at any time. He wanted to be ready.

Jonah raised his eyebrows at Eliza as he watched his mom and dad haggle with an old lady selling shiny purses. They had been the ones who suggested the trip into the city, a final day of summer fun before school started.

"Really, Mom? New York?" he had said, trying to plead with his eyes. *You do remember what happened there last time, don't you?*

"Jonah," she had said lovingly. "We can't live in fear, now, can we?"

He had come without complaint, but the feeling he had today made him wonder if they would all regret the decision.

Up ahead, Eleanor motioned for them to hurry up. As they turned the corner after her, the crowd grew noticeably thicker.

Benjamin Stone grabbed seven-year-old Jeremiah and lifted him up onto his shoulders.

"Whoa!" Jeremiah said. "Check out the parade!"

Jonah craned his neck around the tall couple in front of him. When he saw the participants in the parade, he breathed in sharply. Bloodred lanterns hung from wires across the street, and a line of what looked like giant, twisted puppets moved in a circle. Awful faces that made him think immediately of the Fallen, on top of pencil-thin necks, stretching high above the crowd.

The scene made him feel even more uneasy.

An explosion went off overhead, causing Jonah to throw his arms up over his face. A shower of blue light cascaded down all around them.

"Relax, Jonah," his mom said, smiling. "It's just a Chinese festival and some fireworks."

Eliza and Jeremiah giggled at him.

"Yeah, I know," he mumbled, stuffing his hands into his pockets. "Isn't it about time to go?"

"You want to leave during the fireworks display?" Benjamin

laughed. "Come on, Jonah. Just hang in there for a few more minutes."

He started to protest but was distracted by a young woman walking along the sidewalk, against the crowd. Her blonde hair was pulled back in a ponytail, and for a second before she passed by, she turned toward Jonah.

She smiled a small, knowing smile, and her green eyes pierced him like icicles.

Then, for the briefest moment, they shimmered yellow.

Jonah sucked in his breath as he turned to watch her. She quickly disappeared around the corner behind them. He felt his legs begin to move in her direction, almost on their own, and before he knew it, he was following her, his eyes darting everywhere at once in search of the fallen one.

He reached the corner and peeked around, only to see a blonde ponytail turn into a doorway. Glancing back, he saw his family still caught up in the fireworks display. No one had noticed that he was gone.

He felt his breathing quicken as he crouched down, his back against the wall. Nine months ago, he and Eliza had entered the hidden realm for the first time. Now it had become almost second nature. He remembered what Henry, his family's guardian angel, had said about entering—that it took two things: being an angel, of course. And then, heartfelt belief.

If only Henry were here now. He'd been promoted to warrior-class angel after he helped Jonah and Eliza rescue the kidnapped nephilim, including their mom, and return them to their families. Jonah was happy for Henry, and they even had a new guardian angel now, Cassandra. But she was just learning the ropes and kept to herself a lot. Jonah couldn't help sometimes feeling like the responsibility for his family's safety was now entirely on his own shoulders. He took a few deep breaths, trying to calm his racing heart as he lowered his head.

"I believe in You, Elohim," he prayed quietly. "And in the reality of the spiritual world, the real world behind everything else. I believe in the hidden realm."

Anyone watching would have thought that Jonah had disappeared, but he had just slipped into the hidden realm. Jonah opened his eyes and stood up. The street and the buildings all looked the same to him, but it was the people in the hidden realm that always took his breath away. They had an electric glow about them, some like a dim, fading chunk of charcoal, while others, a brilliant white. He moved as fast as he could down the street, trying to avoid running into anyone. Even though they couldn't see him, he could pass through them. But the electric jolt Jonah experienced when he did always made him cringe.

The woman had turned into an alleyway with a sign overhead that read CHINATOWN ARCADE. He peered inside, expecting to see kids playing video games. But there were no games there. Instead, he saw a long, smoky tunnel, with doors to shops along the walls on each side, and a handful of men standing and talking quietly, some of them leaning against the brick walls.

Down the dark corridor, Jonah saw the ponytailed girl again. He paused, his mind replaying the scene on the street. *Her eyes had flashed yellow, right?* He blinked twice, then slowly reached behind his shoulder. An arrow appeared in his fingertips, and as he extended his left arm, a bow appeared. He leveled it at her and took aim.

He was about to release it when he felt a hand grab his shoulder.

"Jonah! Wait!"

He turned back to see Eliza, wide-eyed and panting, the glow around her heart telling him she had entered the hidden realm too.

"Look closer," she said, nodding toward the girl. "And just . . . take a deep breath or something."

Jonah squinted in the darkness and slowly dropped his arrow. He could see the faint glow coming from the girl. Then a figure pushed off the wall and reached out to her. She took his hand, and Jonah heard her giggle.

She was no fallen angel.

"But her eyes . . . ," he mumbled. "They turned yellow, like all of *theirs* are."

They watched as the couple exited the other side of the corridor.

Eliza cocked her head to the side. "Maybe a reflection from the fireworks?"

Jonah's gaze lingered toward the doorway for a few more long seconds as he wondered how he could have almost shot a human with an arrow.

"Where are we?" asked Eliza.

Suddenly they heard a woman's voice calling out from somewhere beyond the alleyway opening. It was faint, but clear, as if the words had been whispered directly into Jonah's ears. But it was clear they had traveled a very long way. "There is a spiritual realm behind the reality that you see. Behind this street, these buildings, this world!"

"Do you hear that?" Jonah said, not waiting for Eliza to answer. He began to move toward the voice.

At the opening to the alley, he saw cars zooming by and people moving up and down the sidewalks. But the accented voice carried above it all.

"The spiritual realm is more real than these cars, the sidewalk, this cart of ginger root. Praise be to Elohim, the King of kings!"

A tall, dark-skinned woman wearing a brightly colored batik dress and a scarf around her hair stood on the corner across the street from them. She held a microphone that was connected to a small stereo speaker. She waved her hand in the air as she spoke.

"No one seems to be listening," said Eliza. The swarm of people moving along the street avoided her like rushing water around a boulder. Neither the locals nor the tourists paid her any attention.

Jonah, however, found himself riveted to the street preacher's commanding voice.

"There is a battle raging. Not between the United States and the Middle East. Not between Christians and Muslims. This is not a battle of flesh and blood! Ephesians 6. It is a battle between good and evil, between the spiritual forces of darkness and those of the Light! It is waged not with missiles and might, but on your knees in prayer to the almighty One! And whether you know it or not, you are choosing sides right now.

"Think carefully, my friends. Joshua 24. 'Choose this day whom you will serve. Will it be the gods your ancestors served? As for me and my house, we will serve the Lord!'"

Jonah felt his heart leap inside his chest as he listened to her words.

She stood still as people continued to wander by, paying her no mind. Her eyes moved back and forth across the crowd as she caught her breath. Then she looked across the street and paused as if she saw something unexpected.

The thing was, she seemed to be looking right at Jonah and Eliza.

Eliza leaned toward him and spoke out of the side of her mouth. "She's acting like she can see us, don't you think? But we're still . . . you know . . ."

"In the hidden realm," Jonah said, finishing her thought. "I know."

The woman's eyes were locked on them, though. What started as surprise now turned into a smile, and she began to nod her head slightly. Closing her eyes for a moment, she turned her head upward and raised both her hands to the sky, as if receiving a new message to speak.

Jonah felt his heart growing warmer somehow. He looked down at his chest. Not only did it feel warmer, but he seemed to be glowing steadily brighter.

The street preacher opened her mouth again, her eyes still trained on them. Jonah snapped to attention.

"Listen! Romans 9. 'Does not the potter have the right to make out of the same lump of clay some pottery for special purposes and some for common use?' There are those among us who are indeed uncommon . . ."

Jonah glanced at Eliza and raised his eyebrows.

"Those whom Elohim has created for a special purpose. Do not fear, my friends! Elohim is sending His warriors to do battle on our behalf. Giving their allegiance to Him and His Son, they will do battle with the principalities, the powers of darkness— indeed, with Abaddon himself. He will strike his blows, but thanks be to God, in the name of Jesus, they will thwart him."

Jonah heard only her words now, no honking horns or old women selling vegetables or young men calling out to one another. Everything else faded away as he stared into the woman's penetrating brown eyes.

"And one of these servants, although young, will be a thorn in the side of the Evil One. Pray for him, my friends. Dark days are ahead. He must resist the devil and follow Elohim alone, or risk the fall of many."

The African woman stood in silence, eyes locked on Jonah's, any hint of a smile now gone. After a long moment she shook her head to herself and turned away.

"Hey!" Jonah called out. "Can you see us? Can I talk to you for a minute?" He began to run across the street, passing through a mob of people, feeling a barrage of electric jolts but not caring.

Jonah reached the other side, but she was gone. Somehow the tall woman in the colorful dress had already disappeared among the hundreds of people on the sidewalks.

Eliza was right behind him, but she couldn't find the street preacher either.

Neither of them saw the figure standing in the darkness behind the flow of people, one building over. He watched them for another minute with his yellow eyes. Finally, he turned, flapped his crusty wings once, and shot off into a moonless sky.

TWO

BOYS' BATHROOM BATTLE

F inally!" Eliza said, hopping off the bus and moving quickly past Jonah and toward the school.

"Calm down," Jonah called out, slightly annoyed. "It's just sixth grade."

She spun back toward him. "*Calm down?* It's the *first day* of sixth grade, and probably the most exciting day of my twelve-year-old life! We get to find out all about our new teachers and classes and lockers . . . and new books!"

"Hey," Jonah said quietly, brushing off her enthusiasm. "Did you see Cassandra this morning?"

"You mean Cassandra, the mysteriously disappearing guardian angel?" Eliza said with a laugh. "No, but that's not too unusual, is it?"

He hesitated, but then nodded. He was still used to seeing Henry all the time, and it was true, their new guardian angel hadn't been as obvious about her presence. This morning was probably just another example.

Jonah walked into the school with a few busloads of other students, high-fiving a few friends he hadn't seen all summer, all of them with the same triumphant look on their faces. *Eighth grade. Finally!*

He turned down a hallway to the right and found himself in the middle of lockers slamming and kids chatting excitedly. The eighth-grade hall. As he was about to find his locker, he saw Susie Dickerson and her friend Melissa walking right toward him. His heart jumped a little bit into his throat as they made eye contact.

"Have you gotten taller, Jonah?" Susie asked, smiling. Jonah felt his face growing hotter. He had grown four full inches over the summer. Eliza had grown three.

He tried to think of something clever to say. "Yeah, uh—" But as he began to move toward them, he felt someone kick his right foot. It hit the back of his left leg, and suddenly he was sprawled out on the floor.

"Welcome to eighth grade, Stone!" Zack Smellman and his two friends, Peter Snodgrass and Carl Fong, laughed hysterically. Before Jonah could pick himself up, they walked off through the crowd of kids who had now turned to see for themselves who had ended up on the ground.

Jonah fumed. He could tear them apart if he wanted to, stuff them inside a locker or worse. And after he stopped them from beating up a little kid the year before, they all knew it. It was probably a good thing that they had walked away so fast. The words his father often said pried their way into his head once again. If he wanted to have a normal school life, he couldn't afford to reveal his true abilities. He had to keep a low profile and, above all, control his temper.

The girls stifled laughs of their own and waved at him as they hurried by. *Great start to the school year,* Jonah thought as he gathered his things.

Based on the first five minutes of his geometry class, he realized that school was going to be a lot harder than last year. He already had an hour and a half of homework and had been to only one class.

Next up was history, one of Jonah's favorite subjects, with Mrs. Larson. He found a desk in the middle of the room, plopped his backpack down, and took out a notebook and pencil. Two tall kids came in and walked toward the back of the room—Peter Snodgrass and Carl Fong. *Wonderful,* Jonah thought. Even without Zack Smellman goading them along, Snodgrass and Fong were no picnic. Jonah ground his teeth as both of them "accidentally" knocked him with their book bags as they passed by.

But Jonah was determined not to cause a scene on his first day of school. If he could make it through most of seventh grade without pounding any faces, he could make it through his first day of eighth grade. Jonah unclenched his fists and quickly turned his attention to his new history teacher, who had started lecturing on the Civil War.

When class was over and he had another hour's worth of homework and a new, heavy history book to carry around, Jonah took a minute to go to the boys' restroom. He chose a stall and closed himself in.

He heard the door to the bathroom open, and then slam shut. *Click.*

Did someone just lock the door?

Footsteps shuffled across the tiled floor. Jonah tried to peek through the crack in the stall to see who was in there with him.

There were eight stalls in the bathroom, and he was in the

third. He didn't hear anyone talking, but he heard the first door slam open. Like someone had kicked it in. The same thing happened with door number two.

Someone began to speak in a hushed, singsong voice. "Come on out, Jonah Stone. We know you're in here." A chill ran up his spine as Jonah felt his locked door get pushed. "And we know exactly who you aaaaaaaare."

If they didn't have Jonah's attention before, they had it now.

But no one outside of the family knew who he was. Who he *really* was—that he was only three-quarters human. And neither of his siblings would share their family secret with anybody . . . would they?

Don't overreact, Jonah. This has to be some kind of misunderstanding. No need to freak out.

"Who . . . who are you? What do you want? I'm kind of . . . ah . . . busy here."

There was no pause. The door slammed against him, ripped off its hinges. A long arm reached in and grabbed Jonah, pulling him out of the stall and throwing him against the cold floor.

Standing above him, with dull eyes but smug smiles, were Peter Snodgrass and Carl Fong.

Jonah was about to get on his feet and show these two what the son of a nephilim could do when suddenly over Fong's shoulder a black-winged creature appeared, its fingers curled around the boy's arm, its face close to his ear. At the same time, another one materialized over Snodgrass.

He could see them. Had he entered the hidden realm? No. Angels could be seen in the physical world, but only if they chose to be. Another chill ran down Jonah's spine. These creatures were announcing their presence to him. They *wanted* to be seen.

"Go on," one of them hissed into Snodgrass's ear. "It's time to get revenge for what happened last year."

"Yes, yes!" the other cooed. "Show this kid what happens when losers try to be heroes!"

Jonah wasn't sure if the boys could see or hear the creatures or if they could tell that it was the creatures who were encouraging them to fight, but it didn't matter right now. Their fists began to rise, and he knew that if he didn't make a move soon, the only way he'd be getting off this bathroom floor was with a mop.

Jonah jumped to his feet and grabbed Fong by the shoulders, throwing him across the room with his angelic strength. Then he ducked as Snodgrass swung his fist toward Jonah's face, driving his foot into the boy's middle and sending him in the same direction as his friend. They both slammed against the wall and fell splayed across the tiled floor.

The creatures shrieked and jumped off the boys' shoulders. Their horrible faces were wrenched and contorted, sharp teeth protruding from their open mouths, crusty black wings flapping wildly on their backs. And those awful eyes.

They moved toward him as he felt his back press up against the cold wall. He glanced toward the locked door but was pretty sure he was too far away to make a run for it. He would have to fight both of them to get out of here. Jonah said a silent prayer to Elohim and slipped into the hidden realm to fight. If someone did somehow get past the locked door, it would be better if he didn't have to explain why he was apparently having an imaginary battle next to two unconscious students.

"Okay," he said, swallowing hard. "I guess it's just you guys and me. I'm warning you, though—you're gonna get disintegrated all over this dirty boys' bathroom floor."

Jonah reached his right hand across his left hip and pulled. In his hand appeared a long, silvery-white blade. An angelblade. Given to him by the archangel Michael himself.

The two fallen ones reached back and pulled fiery arrows off their backs in unison, leveling them at Jonah's chest. But suddenly, something pulled their attention away from him. Their eyes were drawn past Jonah toward the window, and their smiles faded instantly.

As Jonah held up his sword, he saw in its reflection what had drawn their attention. A face had appeared at the window, and it looked angry. Suddenly, the window smashed, glass scattered across the floor, and the creature whose face Jonah had seen flew into the room. More of them pushed themselves through the now-gaping hole. One after the other, they leaped to the floor and stood behind Jonah.

Jonah spun around, expecting to see more enemies. Instead, he saw a dozen warrior-class angels standing in the bathroom, blades and bows drawn, glaring menacingly at the Fallen. Jonah felt himself standing taller now and turned to face the two fallen angels again.

The Fallen took a step back, but instead of retreating, they let their weapons fly. The flame-tipped arrows bounced off the angels' shields and crashed into the walls in different directions, extinguishing, then disappearing into nothing.

The angels quickly unsheathed their blades and advanced on the fallen ones. An explosion of heat and light surrounded them as they made fast work of their enemies. One of the angels slammed a fallen one against the sink. A pipe burst, and water began to spew everywhere. Within seconds, the floor was covered with both water and black dust, the only evidence that fallen angels had been there. Jonah was showered by the spray and watched breathlessly as chunks of the dust floated around the floor.

They weren't dead. Angels—good or bad—don't just die. But they were gone, at least for now, and that was enough.

"Thanks," Jonah said to the angels. He stood for a moment in the spewing stream of water, eyeing them. Their silver armor glistened brightly, their wings razor sharp, faces chiseled. It was hard not to just stare at them in awe. "How did you know I was in trouble?"

A shorter, stocky angel with blond, spiky hair replied, "No time for that now, Jonah. We need to find your brother and sister. They are in great danger."

"Eliza and Jeremiah too?" Jonah asked.

The angel nodded.

"Abaddon wants all of you dead."

THREE

OUTSIDE
MRS. LITTLE'S ROOM

Jonah prayed again and returned to the physical realm before emerging from the boys' bathroom, along with the water that was beginning to seep under the door. His shoes squished with every step he took. The bell had sounded, and the few lingering students scurried toward their classrooms. One girl who rushed past him saw the water and turned to stare at the soaked kid coming out of the bathroom. Jonah lowered his head and walked away as fast as he could.

The troop of angels followed closely behind, invisible to the other students. Their eyes scanned the hallway for any sign of more fallen angels.

Elohim, Jonah prayed silently as he moved down the hallway, *please protect Eliza and Jeremiah. Keep them safe until we get there.*

He uttered the prayer over and over as he made his way toward the second-grade hall.

The angel in command sent half of the troops toward the sixth-grade wing in search of Eliza.

Jonah and the rest continued toward Jeremiah's classroom. If Jeremiah had to face fallen angels like the ones Jonah did, he wouldn't stand a chance. Jonah moved as fast as he could without running, for fear of attracting too much attention. His wet shoes were already loud enough. Not to mention the dripping.

He turned the corner toward Mrs. Little's room. The hallway was empty. He passed by rooms and saw second graders busily working at their desks. How exactly was he going to get to his brother?

The angels marched silently behind him, but as far as anyone else knew, he was in the hallway alone.

Peering through the skinny window on Jeremiah's classroom door, he saw his brother. All of the other kids were sitting at their desks, working. But Jeremiah stood beside his, trying to balance a pencil on his nose. Two girls watching had their hands on their mouths and were giggling.

Typical, Jonah thought. *Always looking for an audience.*

He cleared his throat and put his hand on the doorknob. Just as he did, though, he noticed two figures at the end of the hallway. He looked up and saw two kids who looked like teenagers, a boy and a girl. They locked their yellow eyes onto Jonah's. He glanced back at the lead angel, who nodded his head and turned his attention toward the two.

Jonah swallowed hard. He didn't have much time.

He pushed Mrs. Little's door open too hard and it slammed against the wall. All of the kids, as well as the teacher, jumped in unison, startled by the interruption. Mrs. Little, who had been writing math problems on the whiteboard, put her hand on her chest.

"For goodness' sake, Jonah Stone!" she said. "You almost gave me a heart attack! What on earth are you—?"

"I need Jeremiah," Jonah interrupted, ignoring the water dripping from his hair and clothes and onto her floor. He was hoping she would ignore it too. He glanced over his shoulder impatiently as he spoke. "It's . . . our dog," he said, frantically trying to make up an excuse. "He's . . . gone into the hospital . . . er . . . the animal hospital . . . and, well, we need Jeremiah because we don't . . . ah . . . think Fluffy is going to make it."

Mrs. Little took her glasses off and let them hang around her neck, and looked suspiciously at Jonah and the growing puddle of water at his feet.

But Jonah wasn't going to wait for an answer. With twenty pairs of eyes watching his every move, he walked over to Jeremiah's desk.

Squish, squish, squish.

"Come on, Jeremiah," he said hurriedly, looking toward the door again. "We need to go. *Now.*"

"But we don't even have a—" Before Jeremiah could say the word *dog*, Jonah slapped his hand over his brother's mouth and turned his shoulders toward the door.

He forced a smile. "That's right, we need to go take care of our dog. We should have him back by lunchtime, Mrs. Little. Nothing to worry about."

Jeremiah tried to say something with Jonah's hand on his face, but Jonah held on tightly, still smiling and nodding at the teacher, who was at a loss for words.

Jonah slung his brother out into the hallway and shut the door behind him.

"I didn't even get my book bag, Jonah!" his brother said. "And since when do we have a dog? And why are you all wet?"

Jonah wasn't listening. The boy and girl in the hallway had moved closer, and once they saw the brothers come out, they began to walk toward them with purpose.

The angels stood in the hallway too, bracing themselves for another fight.

"Whoa," Jeremiah said, wide-eyed. "Angels! In our school!"

"This way, fast!" Jonah grabbed his arm and dragged him in the opposite direction, down the hall and away from the approaching kids.

"But . . ." Jeremiah tried to protest but couldn't get away from Jonah's superstrong grip.

Jonah was about to start running when a voice called out from around the corner that made him stop in his tracks.

"Jonah Stone!"

The voice boomed off the lockers in the hallway. A huge, hulking man stepped out in front of them, standing in the middle of their path, with his fists on his hips. He was the size of a professional football offensive lineman.

That was because this man used to *be* an offensive lineman. It was Mr. Anderson, the principal of Granger Community School.

He pointed a finger from one of his huge meat-slab hands at Jonah. "Son, I need to see you in my office immediately. We need to talk about why the eighth-grade boys' bathroom is flooding out into the hallway."

Jonah pushed his hair out of his face, rubbing sweat off his brow. He stood, still holding Jeremiah's arm, and looked back again. The presence of the principal had caused the boy and girl to stop, at least momentarily. They stood with their arms crossed, smirking, eyes smoldering. The looks on their faces delivered a single, awful message. *We're going to kill you.*

Jonah was frozen. Which way should he go? There was another fight waiting if they went toward the fallen angels disguised as teenagers. But the idea of going with the principal didn't seem much better. They'd be safe for a while. But how was he going to explain why the bathroom was spewing water?

"Well?" Mr. Anderson said impatiently. "What are you waiting for? The police to show up?"

The angels had quietly changed their position. They now stood in a circle around Jonah and Jeremiah, facing outward. Jonah's eyes met the commander's, who nodded confidently at him.

Jonah knew what he had to do.

Mr. Anderson began walking toward them.

So did the fallen angels.

Jonah bowed his head and focused all of his thoughts on Elohim.

"Jeremiah," he whispered, "I need you to do exactly as I say. Can you handle that?"

"What?" his brother said. Jonah squeezed his arm tightly. "That hurts!"

"Listen," Jonah said. "Say this prayer with me. And I want you to mean it, okay?"

Jeremiah was caught by the tone in his brother's voice. "Okay."

Jonah murmured the words quickly, and Jeremiah closed his eyes and repeated them.

Suddenly, he and Jeremiah disappeared from sight.

FOUR

A Short Flight Home

"How . . . what . . . where . . . ?"

Mr. Anderson stood, staring at the empty space in the hallway that had been occupied a few seconds ago by Jonah and Jeremiah Stone. He blinked a few times, then noticed the unfamiliar teenage boy and girl a little farther away, who were moving toward him rapidly. "And where do you two think you're going?"

Neither one answered. They simply disappeared just as Jonah and Jeremiah had done moments before.

Mr. Anderson stood dumbfounded, running his fingers through his hair. Then a jolt hit his body, like an electrical current, causing him to jump.

Jonah could have passed around Mr. Anderson, but he couldn't resist giving the principal a little shock. He still had Jeremiah by the arm, and now that they were in the hidden realm, he continued to pull him along. The angels followed closely behind.

Before they turned the corner, Jonah glanced back in time to see that the two teens who had been following him had morphed into enormous fallen angels now that they were in the hidden realm. The fallen began to charge down the hallway, pulling arrows off their backs.

Three of the angels protecting Jonah and Jeremiah stopped running, turned around, and began to fire their arrows.

Jonah had no time to stick around for a fight. Not if they were going to make sure Eliza was okay and get out of there.

"Where are we going, Jonah?" asked Jeremiah, trying to move his shorter legs fast enough to keep up.

"We have to go find Eliza, now!" he barked at his brother. "I'll explain it later. Just come on!"

Jonah, Jeremiah, and the three remaining angels ran toward the sixth-grade classrooms as the bell rang and students began pouring into the hallway. As was always true in the hidden realm, each person they passed had a glow. A dull glow in some. In others, here and there, the bright glow of a life given to Elohim.

Jonah's heart was racing. What was going on? Why were they being attacked? He found himself praying silently as they moved down the hallway. *Elohim, please protect Eliza and my parents.*

Turning down the sixth-grade hall, Jonah and Jeremiah arrived just in time to see an angel fire an arrow into a screeching fallen one, who disintegrated into dust on the floor. Eliza's glowing shield of faith was surrounding her and a group of angels, but there were no more of the Fallen in sight, and Jonah watched as she lowered it. Her ability to create the shield of faith had appeared when Jonah and Eliza were rescuing their mother. She had learned to summon it by raising her hands in the air and focusing her mind and heart on Elohim.

"Eliza!" Jonah called out, running over, followed by Jeremiah and the rest of the angels. "Are you okay?"

Eliza nodded. "Sure, now that the fallen angels are gone."

"Yeah," said Jonah. "I got attacked in the boys' bathroom. If it wasn't for these angels . . ." He didn't want to say it out loud. He wouldn't be here right now.

"Me too," she said. "I was just getting ready to go to my locker when these guys came at me out of nowhere." Eliza turned toward the angels. "Thanks." They bowed their heads slightly in return.

"Jonah?" said the commanding angel, tapping his finger on the hilt of his sword.

Jonah nodded. "We need to go, Eliza. It's not safe here. There may be others."

"You mean, leave school?" she said.

Jonah rolled his eyes. Even when they were under attack, the thought of missing even one minute of school had her worried.

"It's just the first day, Eliza," he said impatiently. "You've got all year to be here. But today, we need to get home."

Jeremiah was still watching the dust on the floor that used to be a fallen angel. Jonah grabbed his hand as they turned to leave.

"Come on, Jeremiah," he said. "Time to go home."

Jeremiah nodded his head but continued to look back over his shoulder at the remnants of the fallen angel. He had seen Elohim's angels before, but never one of the Fallen, and he hadn't discovered any of his powers yet. Jonah was sure Jeremiah was scared that he wouldn't be able to stop the Fallen if they came after him again.

But they had to hurry. They ran down the hallway, carefully looking around each corner for signs of Elohim's enemies. They made it to the front of the school, past the offices, and stood together outside the main entrance.

Jeremiah finally spoke up, his voice trembling slightly. "Those were . . . fallen angels?"

Jonah saw the angels looking out in all directions around them for signs of more trouble. He rested his hands on his knees, bending over toward his brother, who stared up at him with wide eyes.

"There are bad angels out there, Jeremiah," he said as calmly as he could. "They turned their back on Elohim, and now, well . . . they don't like it when anybody follows Him."

Jeremiah bit his lower lip for a few seconds, letting that sink in. He looked back up at Jonah with his clear blue eyes. "They want to kill us?"

Jonah tried to smile. "We have angels here to help us. And look, we're not totally defenseless. Kids like us—quarterlings— have special gifts."

"I don't," he said matter-of-factly and folded his arms across his chest.

Jonah put his hand behind his brother's head and pulled him close. "You will. You just have to be patient, that's all."

One of the angels had approached them. "Time to fly, kids."

"Fly? With you guys?" Jeremiah asked.

The angel extended his hand. "How 'bout you ride with me, young Jeremiah?"

A small smile creased Jeremiah's mouth for the first time since he'd been pulled from his class. "Okay," he said, beaming up at the angel.

"Oh brother," Eliza said, who'd been busy patrolling with the angels. She hated flying. It always made her feel sick to her stomach.

"Oh, come on, Eliza," Jonah said, holding on to the angel beside him. "Just think of it like . . . a ride at an amusement park."

"I don't like rides at amusement parks!" she yelled as the angel she held on to lifted off the ground.

They soared through the air, over the trees, held aloft by the angels. Jonah watched as the cars became smaller and smaller. Over to his left was Jeremiah with his right arm stretched out, away from the angel. To his right was Eliza, with her jaws clenched and lines creasing her face, tightly clutching her angel.

Jonah's mind churned through the battle at school, hoping when they arrived home there would be some answers waiting for them.

From this distance, above everything, it was hard to imagine that any battle raged at all. Peacefield looked quiet, sleepy. Moms were out with their little ones in strollers. Joggers ran up and down the streets.

No one seemed to have any idea what was happening around them or what might be lurking around any corner. Jonah considered this as they flew along. *If only they could see what we just saw. Then they would know.*

"Look, Jonah, look!" Jeremiah pointed excitedly toward their home, the small white house on Cranberry Street.

Lining the roof of their house stood a battalion of angels. More than Jonah had ever seen. Across their front lawn were more, forming an angelic perimeter around the house. As they approached, Jonah saw their determined faces, their bodies standing rigidly at attention, arrows strung or hands resting on the hilts of their swords.

Jonah, Eliza, and Jeremiah landed on their driveway, and two angels stepped aside briefly to allow them to pass through.

Jonah turned to the commanding angel. "What's really going on here?"

"My orders are to get you into the house safely," he said, moving Jonah and the others toward the door. "I'm sure you'll get your answers inside."

If Henry were here, he would have some answers for me, Jonah thought, but he bit his tongue and didn't say anything. There was no use snapping at their protectors. Before Jonah, Eliza, and Jeremiah could reach their front door, Eleanor burst outside and came running toward them.

"Jonah! Eliza!" she cried out as she pulled them close to her. "Jeremiah! Let me look at you." She held each of their faces in her hands and looked them over until she was satisfied that they were all unharmed.

"Mom, we're all fine," Jonah said. "We didn't have too much trouble. The angels were a lot of help." The commanding angel eyed him and raised his eyebrow at Jonah's attempt to downplay the attacks, but said nothing.

"You three better come on inside," she said. "We need to talk."

"Good," Eliza said, pushing her glasses up her nose and glancing at Jonah. "Because I have some questions."

They hurried through their front door and were immediately grabbed by their dad, Benjamin, in a big bear hug.

"I'm so glad you're okay," he said as calmly as he could manage. "We've been praying as hard as we could ever since the angels let us know what was going on. We wanted to come get you ourselves this morning. But Taryn and Marcus wouldn't allow it."

Before Jonah could say anything, Eliza squealed.

"Henry!"

Their former guardian angel stood in the living room. His usual T-shirt and jeans were replaced by full-fledged angelic armor.

He was covered in silvery metallic gear from head to toe. But his face wore the same grin he always had.

"Eliza! Boys!" He nodded. "I'm glad to see you're all doing okay."

She ran to hug him, and he blushed but hugged her back.

"Hey, Henry," Jonah said quietly. Seeing him for the first time since he'd left made him feel weird. They had become really good friends, and then Henry had ditched him and his whole family.

"Jonah," said Henry warmly. He held up his hand. Jonah hesitated but finally slapped a high five with his former guardian angel.

Beside him stood two angels, one of them enormous and muscular, the other a female, lean and sleek, with a blaze of red hair.

"Marcus. Taryn." Jonah walked over and greeted the angels they had met last year when their mother was kidnapped.

Eliza stepped forward now, unable to contain herself any longer. "Does someone want to tell us what is going on? I was almost attacked at school by fallen angels."

"I *was* attacked," Jonah said. "In the boys' bathroom, right after they sent two of the school's bullies after me. If the angels hadn't come, I would have been toast."

"They were after me too," said Jeremiah. "I saw them, Mom, the black angels with the yellow eyes." He reached out for Eleanor's hand and grabbed it, drawing close to her. She leaned down and placed an arm around his chest.

"Attacks on nephilim and quarterlings have taken place today across the world," Taryn said. "Probably entirely undetected by humans. We were tipped off when we lost contact with your guardian angel."

"You haven't heard from Cassandra?" asked Eliza. "Is she okay?"

"We're not sure yet," Taryn said. "You can imagine, of course, that we keep close tabs on the nephilim and their families after what happened last year. When Cassandra didn't file her daily report this morning, we grew concerned. When the other guardian angels didn't either . . ."

"We sounded the alarm," said Marcus. "We believe that these were coordinated efforts by Abaddon and his forces."

Jonah's mind churned. "What are they trying to do?"

Taryn glanced at Marcus. "We're not entirely sure, Jonah. But we have sent angelic forces to each nephilim family around the world, just like here. Based on what we know, it makes sense to assume that they are trying to rid the world of the nephilim."

"And their children," added Marcus, without a hint of emotion in his voice.

The room grew silent. Jonah felt his heart begin to beat faster. The reality hit him that his entire family was in danger.

The phone rang and reluctantly Benjamin picked it up across the hallway in his office. Jonah's ears perked up when he heard him say, "Good morning to you, Mr. Anderson."

"Yes, he's here . . . Yes . . . No . . ." He paused, listening. And then, "You think my son flooded the boys' bathroom?!" Benjamin was pacing around his desk now, a sure sign that he was getting angry. "I understand, Mr. Anderson, that he may have been seen walking out of the bathroom as it happened, but there has to be some kind of . . ." He paused again. "The police? You think he's a *vandal*? You have to be kidding . . . Yes, yes, okay. It really doesn't matter at this . . . well, never mind. I'll speak with him, and we'll talk to them when they get here. And we will be speaking with you again as well—understand? Good-bye." Jonah's dad hung up the phone.

"Dad?" Jonah watched his father take off his glasses and massage his forehead.

"It's, uh . . . it's really not a big deal, considering everything now." He gave a hollow laugh. "They think you flooded the boys' bathroom on purpose. They have witnesses who say they saw you run out. He's suspending you from school until this matter can be sorted out." Benjamin replaced his glasses with one hand and patted Jonah on the shoulder with the other. "One more thing— the police are on their way to pick you up. For vandalizing school property. I think he's overreacting a bit."

Eleanor had her hands on her hips. "You *think*?"

Jonah put both of his hands on his head as his mind spun. His life was over.

But Eliza's voice broke through his thoughts. "Well, I'm sorry to have to bring you all back to reality, but if Abaddon is after our very lives, Jonah getting accused of flooding the bathroom is the least of our worries."

"Agreed." Benjamin nodded. "It just means we have to act fast. The police are on the way, after all."

Taryn spoke up. "As I was saying, we can assume that the nephilim and their families have been attacked, or are about to be. How successful our forces have been at protecting them, we won't know for a while."

Marcus nodded. "One thing's for sure. You are no longer safe here, and we need to get going."

"What exactly do you mean? Are we moving?" asked Jonah. "When? Where?"

Taryn looked at him squarely.

"Now. New York City."

FIVE

THE PEACEFIELD CITY DUMP

Benjamin turned the old white Subaru station wagon so hard around the corner that the tires screeched, and the suitcases slammed around in the back. Jonah had packed so fast, he'd only had time to grab a handful of clothes. After turning his room upside down, he had finally found the Bible Mrs. Aldridge had given him and the silver watch he'd used on his mission to rescue his mom.

"Slow down!" Eleanor cried out, holding on to her armrest. "They're not following us!" Marcus and Taryn had seen to that, sending a few angels to lift the police cruiser just millimeters off the ground so its tires couldn't get any traction.

He waved his hand in the air. "Sorry, everyone." But he punched the gas again hard, zooming past the school where the Stone kids had been attacked less than an hour before.

Eleanor sat beside him, with Jonah, Eliza, and Jeremiah in the backseat. They held on to each other and the door handles as their dad drove wildly down the street.

"Don't you think you're going to draw more attention to us driving like this?" Eleanor said pointedly.

Benjamin shrugged. "Maybe," he said, and let his foot off the gas slightly. "But we just need to get there as fast as we can." He kept shifting his eyes from the road ahead to the rearview mirror, back and forth.

Jonah finally had a chance to catch his breath. "So, New York? We're really going back there?"

"How can that possibly be safer than Peacefield?" Eliza jumped in.

Jeremiah held Eliza's hand tightly, biting his lower lip, clearly trying not to cry.

Jonah was thinking the same thing Eliza was. New York was where they had entered the hidden realm for the first time, where the battle between good and evil takes place. Where Abaddon was gathering all of his awful strength to fight Elohim. Jonah remembered all the creatures they had faced and almost lost their lives to. How could that place possibly be better than the place they were leaving?

Eleanor looked out her window as she spoke. "We have to trust Elohim," she said simply. "And that these friends of ours out there know what they're doing."

Jonah looked out the window and up. He saw the power lines and clouds zooming by, but he also saw a band of angels flying above them, encircling the car. He was comforted by the fact that they were riding with more protection than a presidential secret service escort. Warrior angels from the Second Battalion of the Angelic Forces of the West were their front and rear guard.

Henry was part of the circle, flying right above him. Jonah

caught his eye and waved. His former guardian angel saw him and smiled slightly, then returned his focus to his task.

"He looks good up there in his battle gear, don't you think?" Eliza said, leaning over Jonah to take a look.

Jonah looked at her and snorted. Eliza turned a dark shade of pink and hit him in the stomach. "You know what I mean. He looks like he . . . belongs up there, with them."

He was about to hit her back when he saw Henry turn his head sharply backward and focus on something behind the car. Jonah looked through the rear window but saw nothing.

Eliza noticed Henry's concerned gaze too. "The hidden realm?" she suggested.

Jonah nodded. They both closed their eyes and in an instant had entered the spiritual world.

Before Jonah could even turn around, he heard the roar of an engine behind them.

Turning now, he quickly realized that it wasn't just the sound of *one* engine. Jonah counted at least six motorcycles on the horizon. They were spread out across two lanes, side by side, and they were closing in on them fast.

Jonah saw his dad's face in the rearview mirror, continuing to focus on the road ahead, unaware of the bikers behind them.

Jonah popped back out of the hidden realm. Eliza had stayed in and was now invisible. "Do you guys see them?"

"You guys just went . . . ?" questioned Jeremiah.

"Into the hidden realm, yes," Jonah said impatiently. "There's an entire motorcycle gang on our tails."

Eleanor glanced back. Jonah saw lines of worry crease her forehead. "Maybe they're just . . . out for a nice ride," she said faintly.

"What are you talking about?" said Benjamin, cutting his eyes up at the rearview mirror. "It's as clear as day back there. I don't see a thing."

"They're in the hidden realm," Jonah muttered. "I'll be back." And with that, he reemerged into the hidden realm with Eliza.

The motorcycles had grown closer, until they were no more than a car length behind. Jonah could see the six riders clearly now, wearing black helmets and dark glasses. A few had leather vests on, while others rode shirtless. Golden bands glistened around each arm and wrist. Every rider had an identical long, thin beard. On their helmets were markings that Jonah faintly recognized.

"Look at their helmets," Eliza said. "Hieroglyphs."

"They're Egyptians?" Jonah said.

Benjamin was clearly getting frustrated, looking back at the two empty seats behind him. "I still don't see anything, guys! Are you sure? Are you even still there?"

"You'd better step on it, dear," answered Eleanor. "Just in case."

In the hidden realm, the Egyptian bikers quickly maneuvered alongside the car until they had it surrounded. The guy on Jonah's side was huge and muscular. He took his index finger, pointed it menacingly at Jonah, and motioned forcefully toward the side of the road.

"It looks like he wants us to pull over," Jonah said.

"Well, that's not going to happen." Eliza scowled as she leaned over to get a better look at the biker. Then she bowed her head and quickly popped back into view of her parents and Jeremiah.

"Go faster, Dad!" she urged their father. "They're completely surrounding us!"

"Hang on, everyone!" Benjamin said, finally convinced that what Jonah and Eliza were seeing was real. He pushed the gas pedal to the floor. They felt the old wagon hesitate and then lurch forward.

Jonah had both hands on the door, turning to watch as they sped past the bikers.

"Nice, Dad!" he shouted, forgetting he was in the hidden realm and Benjamin couldn't hear him. "Keep going!"

"I'm not sure how long this piece of junk can keep going!" said Benjamin. "Where are the angels, for goodness' sake?"

"I'll be back in a minute, guys," Eliza said, then quickly disappeared again.

The bikers had momentarily fallen behind, but with a rev of their engines, they moved back beside them, even closer than before. Benjamin seemed to sense this and punched the gas again, but the car sputtered and didn't move any faster. The speedometer hovered at ninety miles per hour.

"Keep going, Benjamin!" shouted Eleanor. "I think we need to move faster!"

"Come on, car, come on!" Benjamin said, slamming his hand against the steering wheel. "We're going as fast as we can! Where's Henry? Why aren't the angels helping?"

The same biker pulled up beside Jonah again. He motioned to the side of the road once more. This time he pulled back his leather vest. A short golden sword was attached to his side. The biker grinned, exposing a mouthful of golden teeth. He yelled something to Jonah in a foreign language and pointed to the side again.

"No way!" Jonah yelled, and reached back over his head, pulling out a flaming arrow. The bow automatically appeared in his other hand.

Before he could aim it, though, Benjamin slung the car to the left, and then back to the right. The Egyptian bikers moved away, out of the reach of the old wagon.

"I think that's making them angry!" fretted Eliza.

Now, though, the biker closest to Jonah drew his sword. The others did the same. Jonah had no idea what the sword in the hidden realm could do to their car, but they were about to find out unless he could get a straight shot off with his arrow.

Jonah fired as quickly as he could. The biker closest to him leaned backward, the arrow barely missing his chest. The Egyptian grinned and moved in with the weapon.

The metallic ring of a blade echoed through the car, but the biker slumped, turning his front wheel wildly, and fell off the motorcycle.

An angel holding a sword hovered where the biker had been a moment before, looking back as a cloud of black dust flew away on the wind.

"Nice one, guys!" Jonah called up to the angels overhead.

More angels descended to join the sword fight, trying to position themselves between the bikers and the Stones' station wagon, but the Egyptians were tough and giving the angels all they could handle.

"Benjamin!"

Jonah looked ahead of the car. It was Henry, now flying directly in front of them.

"Henry!" called Benjamin. "I see you! What's going on?"

"Follow me, Benjamin!" he called out, pointing ahead. "You're going to have to trust me, okay?"

Benjamin gave him a firm nod, gripping both hands tightly on the wheel and keeping the gas pedal pressed against the floor of the car.

Suddenly, Henry veered off to the right. Benjamin turned the car sharply, leaving the pavement for a bumpy gravel road. The car bounced so hard that their heads crashed into the ceiling.

"Sorry, guys! Hang on!" said their wild-eyed father, intent on following the angel. "Henry told me to stay with him!"

Jonah thought the sign they passed said PEACEFIELD CITY DUMP, but he wasn't sure. He was trying to get another shot off with an arrow, but there was such a battle going on between the angels and the Egyptians that he couldn't get a clean shot. His dad's quick turn had thrown their enemies off, though, and now they were a few feet behind the old wagon.

When he heard his mother scream, his attention was drawn forward again.

They were definitely at the city dump. Massive piles of garbage were visible now directly ahead of them.

But Henry was waving his dad forward. And Benjamin wasn't slowing down.

"Benjamin!" said Eleanor. "We're heading straight for—"

"I know, Eleanor!" But he still didn't slow down or turn.

Then Jonah saw why she was screaming. An enormous mound of smashed metal cars, rusted red, loomed directly in front of them.

Henry seemed to be leading them right toward it.

Jonah and Eliza came back out of the hidden realm now, while Jeremiah was frozen in the seat next to them. Benjamin continued at top speed.

Everything was happening so fast.

Henry looked back at the angels this time, nodding once. Acting as one, they sheathed their swords and sped forward beside him.

Sweat poured down Benjamin's face, but he kept his focus straight ahead.

"This is it, guys!" he said. "This is it!"

Jonah braced himself for a crash. But instead, working so fast they were just a blur, the angels began pushing the cars aside for them. Jonah watched in total amazement as the mountain divided, right in two, and they drove down the middle, barely missing the cars in front of them. The angels held them back and, as soon as their wagon passed, let them go again.

Right on top of the Egyptians.

The clear path for the Stones' car was there for only a flash. Behind them, the cars crashed back down on the ground.

"Woo-hoo!" cried Benjamin.

Jeremiah joined him with a fist pump. "Yes!"

A few more seconds, and they were through the giant mountain of cars, the last one crashing down just behind them as an angel let it go.

Finally, Benjamin took a cue from Henry and slowed the car down, and then stopped. Jonah went into the hidden realm once more but quickly returned.

"They're all gone," he said, eyebrows raised. "Every one of them. Crushed in that mountain of cars. They must have been crushed and disintegrated."

"Just like . . . the Egyptians and the Red Sea," Benjamin said, raising an eyebrow toward Eleanor.

The angels stood in front of the car, giving the Stones a moment to catch their breath.

Jonah breathed out heavily.

Was this going to be their new life? On the run? Just like those ancient Israelites? Were they going to be on Abaddon's hit list for the rest of their lives?

The thought made him shiver. Benjamin must have had the same idea because he turned the car back toward the main road, away from the city dump.

"Keep going fast, Dad," Jonah said. "You never know what else we're going to run into on the way to New York."

SIX

THE SAFE HOUSE

W e're here."

Marcus stopped in front of a collection of older buildings on a quiet side street in central Manhattan. The Stone family set down their bags and looked up at the darkened stone walls and filmy windows. Eliza peered up at the tiled rooftops, shielding her eyes from the sunlight with her hand.

"Looks like we're not the only ones," she said, pointing.

Across the top of each building were dozens of angels, standing guard.

"Wow," said Jonah. He turned to look at the buildings on the other side of the street. They were there too.

"What are those angels doing?" Jeremiah said, wonder in his voice.

Taryn touched the back of his head, smiling. "Standing watch, young friend."

Their eyes returned to the building in front of them. It was dusty and looked old, with a set of heavy wooden doors beneath a large archway.

Across the top of the arch were the words:

CONVENT OF SAINT JOHN OF THE EMPTY TOM

"Convent of Saint John of the Empty . . . *Tom*?" said Jonah. "Who's Tom?"

"It's *tomb*, genius," Eliza answered, rolling her eyes. "Look closely. The *b* is missing."

Jonah squinted. She was right. It was supposed to say *empty tomb*.

"What's a convent?" asked Jeremiah.

Benjamin straightened his glasses. "It's a place where nuns live."

The five of them stood for a minute, staring at the building, angels behind them.

"So," Jonah said, "the safest place for us in New York is in a convent with a bunch of nuns?"

His dad cleared his throat. "It . . . uh . . . appears that way, son."

Marcus walked down the four steps from the street to the entrance.

"The nuns in the Convent of Saint John of the Empty Tomb have graciously offered their help to us. They have always aligned themselves closely with the will and voice of Elohim. You will find no stronger, more faithful women of prayer than these."

Eliza wasn't convinced. "Yeah, but what are they going to do if some Egyptian biker gang shows up? Just . . . pray?"

Taryn laughed lightly. "You have much to learn of the ways of spiritual battle, Eliza."

Jeremiah wrinkled his brow as he looked up at his father. "What's a nun?" he whispered.

"A nun is a woman who has dedicated her whole life to Elohim," Benjamin said patiently. "So much that she doesn't get married, lives with other nuns, and serves the community with them."

Jeremiah thought for a minute. "So you're kind of like a nun, right, Dad? Except that you're married. And you're a dude."

Benjamin cocked his head and squinted at his son with his mouth open, but didn't say anything.

Jonah was the first to follow Marcus inside, finding himself in a small, dank-smelling room. There was a wooden desk in the middle of the space, but no one sitting at it. A hallway stretched out behind it. They stood together in the small foyer and dropped their bags on the floor.

Jonah heard a rumble of whispering voices that seemed to be coming from a room off to the left. He walked over to the doorway and peeked inside.

A circle of women were kneeling together on the floor. Each had on the traditional black-and-white robe and veil. With eyes closed, they were praying.

He watched in silence, enchanted by the display of faithful devotion. Some were kneeling and others were standing, swaying slightly. None of them noticed, or at least acknowledged, Jonah's presence there. They took turns praying softly to Elohim, speaking to Him in a way that Jonah had never heard before. Passionate, loving words that sounded more like talking with a friend than praying to a far-off God. Among the whispers, Jonah heard the words *children*, *protection of Elohim*, and *comfort* multiple times.

"Jonah. What are you—?" Eliza popped into the room beside

Jonah, causing him to jump and blink. She saw the nuns and whispered, "Sorry. I didn't mean to interrupt."

One of the nuns picked her head up, saw Jonah and Eliza standing in the doorway, and quietly stood, leaving the others. She immediately smiled at them, putting Jonah at ease. Her dark skin radiated a glow, and her eyes were full of love.

"Hello, children," she said. "We've been expecting you."

She led them back out into the foyer, where she greeted Benjamin, Eleanor, and Jeremiah as warmly as she had Jonah and Eliza. Apparently Marcus and Taryn hadn't stuck around. Jonah figured they'd gone to catch up with their friends on the roof, or more likely, discuss their strategy and get the latest developments on the attacks.

"It's so nice to meet you all. My name is Sister Patricia. We will do our very best to keep your children safe and sound while you continue your own journey." Turning to Jonah, Eliza, and Jeremiah, she continued, "I'm afraid you won't find our accommodations similar to what you are probably used to. But we do have cozy rooms for you. You'll be bunking with the others, of course."

"What others are you talking about?" asked Jonah, feeling confused.

Sister Patricia gave him a blank look. "The others—the other children. The other ones like you, of course." They continued to stare at her. "No one told you?" She studied the floor, hands on her hips, and sighed loudly. "Well, they really should have filled you in. It's my understanding that you—Benjamin and Eleanor— were merely dropping your children off. It is not safe for the five of you to be together."

Eleanor put her hand over her mouth. Benjamin put a hand on her shoulder in comfort.

"So . . . you guys aren't staying?" As soon as Jeremiah asked the question, Eleanor stifled a sob.

"It'll only be for a little while," whispered Benjamin to his three kids. "If the angels want to keep the nephilim and the quarterlings separate until they get this situation under control, we should trust them. Everything will be all right. I promise."

But something in his father's voice bothered Jonah. He was trying to put a good spin on it, but Jonah had the unsettling feeling that his dad was trying to promise them something that he couldn't be sure of.

Two stone-faced warrior angels approached them in the hallway. They stood silently behind Benjamin and Eleanor.

Benjamin turned and his eyes grew wide. Jonah knew these angels were allowing him to see them now.

"I guess this means it's time for us to go," he said softly. The angels said nothing, but nodded, an urgency on their faces for all to see.

Sister Patricia spoke. "Take a minute and say good-bye to your parents, children."

The five members of the Stone family gathered together in the hall. Benjamin and Eleanor gave multiple hugs to their kids, and Eleanor didn't try to stop the tears now.

"We'll see you soon," she said, wiping them away. "You're safe here, remember? This is . . . the best thing for all of us right now."

Benjamin held her hand in his. "It's time, Eleanor."

She quickly kissed her children once more.

"Okay, Mom, okay," Jonah said, but he hugged her again tightly around her neck, giving her a quick peck on the cheek too.

Benjamin and Eleanor walked down the hallway, under guard of the angels.

Jonah, Eliza, and a sniffling Jeremiah watched them leave until Sister Patricia shut the heavy wooden door, and the sound of the ancient metal latch was a jarring reminder that their parents were gone.

SEVEN

GREETINGS

"Second-floor accommodations are for the sisters of the convent," Sister Patricia said as she led them up the stairwell after dinner, past the door with a large "2" painted on its surface. "Floor three will be for the girls, and floor four will be for the boys," she said.

"So the other kids...they were attacked too?" asked Jeremiah.

The nun smiled thoughtfully at the youngest member of the Stone family. "Yes. One survived an attack on their home in the middle of the night. Another made it through a house fire. I'm sure when they arrive they will be in a bit of shock." She sighed, and Jonah saw pain crease across her face. "But Elohim is Lord, even over days like this. He has a plan."

They walked down the hallway, the dusty wooden floors creaking with each footstep. The nun ushered them past a handful of closed doors, each of them numbered, before she stopped in front of one. Room 312. She looked through a large set of keys.

"Are you the janitor here?" Jeremiah asked, staring enviously at the key ring. Her cheeks creased, and she laughed loudly, the sound echoing down the empty hall.

"No, dear, but you would think so with all of these keys, wouldn't you?"

She opened the door to Eliza's new home. There were two single beds against either wall, a small wooden desk with a chair and lamp, and a small sofa. A worn rug had been placed across the floor. Someone had made an effort with the room, trying to make it comfortable. There just wasn't a lot to work with.

Eliza put on a brave smile and set her bag on the bed. "This will be . . . fine," she said. "Thank you."

"There will be another child who will join you in here eventually," Sister Patricia said. "We don't have enough lodging for everyone to have their own space. It's rare that we ever have this many staying here at one time." She smiled. "Elohim will provide, as He always does."

Eliza nodded, the prospect of a roommate darkening her face. "I'll just take some time to get settled here. You can go ahead and help the boys find their rooms."

The nun nodded. Before she pulled the door closed, she said, "Come down to the main hall at ten thirty in the morning. We'll gather there for some important information and then have a meal."

Jonah wondered what important information they would receive. Maybe they would get an update on the attacks. They walked up one more set of stairs and onto the fourth floor, Jeremiah sticking closely by his side.

"This is the top floor, if you don't count the attic," Sister Patricia said. "You'll be in room 408, Jonah. Third room on the right. It's much like your sister's." She slid a key off her key ring and handed it to him. "Why don't you go on down the hall and get yourself settled? This young man will be in room 420, right here," she said, touching Jeremiah on the shoulder as they stopped in front of his room.

"I'm going to get a roommate too?" Jeremiah said, excitement in his voice. "Just like them? Jonah's my roommate at home."

She patted the top of his head. "Just like Jonah and Eliza, dear."

Jonah left them, continuing down the hallway on his own. The only light came every so often from the small lamps with faded yellow lampshades that were attached to the walls.

He didn't like walking alone down the hall, even if they *were* in a convent. After hurrying to find his room, he was soon sliding the key into the door with 408 on the outside.

His room looked exactly like Eliza's. He threw his book bag onto the floor and flopped himself down on one of the beds.

He tried to relax, but his mind kept playing back the scenes from the day. So much had happened it almost felt like three days had passed.

They'd been attacked, and almost killed, by the forces of Abaddon.

Jonah had been accused of vandalizing the boys' bathroom.

Now they were on the run. They had to fight off a gang of Egyptian bikers from the hidden realm on the way here. Jonah had hoped he would never have to go up against long-dead Bible villains ever again after facing the Leviathan last year on the Brooklyn Bridge. But it seemed Elohim had different plans for him.

And now they were staying with a bunch of nuns, hidden away in New York City.

On top of all those things, they were about to meet a group of kids who were just like them. Who might have the same kinds of powers and abilities.

"There's no telling what's going to happen next," Jonah said to the ceiling of his small room.

Light shone into the room through one small window. He stood and peered out through the blinds. It faced another brick building. Straining to look up, he could just make out the shadow of wings cast by the sunlight onto the brick.

The angels are there.

Somehow, this didn't bring him the comfort he hoped it would. That many angels guarding up above meant that somewhere, down below, fallen angels were plotting their revenge.

PART II

ANGEL SCHOOL

"There is nothing concealed that will not be disclosed,
or hidden that will not be made known."

Matthew 10:26 TNIV

EIGHT

NEW FACES, OLD FRIENDS

Jonah woke with a start at the light knock on the door. He sat up quickly, rubbing his eyes. He looked at his watch, which read 9:38 a.m. The knock came again, and he heard someone outside say, "Hello?"

"Yes?" Jonah said, standing up slowly by the edge of his bed.

The door swung open, and Jonah stood face-to-face with a dark, smiling face. More like face-to-chest, actually. In front of Jonah stood a skinny kid, much taller than him, with an outstretched hand.

"Hello!" the boy, still smiling, said again, with an unfamiliar accent. Jonah, looking up to the boy's face, took his hand and shook it. "Can I come in?"

Jonah moved away from the door. "Yeah, sure, come on in."

The boy had to duck under the door frame to keep from bumping his head. He had an old brown backpack and a couple of worn leather books tied by a cord. He threw these down on the other bed, opposite Jonah's.

"Well, it looks like we are roommates!" he said with enthusiasm. "My name is David. I just arrived here with my sister."

"Jonah," Jonah said, sitting down on the edge of his own bed, running his fingers through his tangled hair, still trying to wake up. David turned toward him and cocked his head to the side.

"Jonah . . . *Stone?*"

David sat down on the bed facing him, his knees higher off the floor than the mattress.

"That's me," he said, wondering why he had said it with that tone. He shifted uncomfortably as David stared at him, finally saying, "What?"

"I'm sorry. I do not mean to stare," David said, barely able to contain his excitement. "It's just that . . . Jonah Stone. Wow . . . In our family, you are a hero!"

Jonah raised his eyebrows at him and felt his face begin to flush red. "A hero?"

"Of course!" said David, standing quickly. He banged his head against the small ceiling fan. "Ow!"

He held his hand on his head, but it did nothing to diminish his enthusiasm.

"I know the whole story," he said, pacing around the small room. "My entire family does! Just last year, how you and your sister saved our mother from the fallen angels. From Abaddon himself!"

Jonah cringed a little, just hearing the name again.

"It was . . . not that big of a deal," he said feebly, eager to get the attention off him.

"Not a big deal?" said David, sitting back down again. He

spoke more softly. "We were heartbroken. We thought we'd never see her again. But you rescued our mother. Elohim used you in a mighty way, my brother. It was a huge deal."

David sat there, smiling, beaming at Jonah, with a grin that stretched his cheeks wide.

"So, uh, where are you from?" asked Jonah, desperately trying to shift the conversation. "Your accent sounds like you're from somewhere in Africa."

"Yes," he said, nodding. "My sister, Ruth, and I are from Uganda. Our father is a doctor in the city of Kampala. Our mother runs an orphanage just outside the city."

His voice radiated pride as he spoke of his family.

"How old are you?" asked Jonah. "You're like . . . six feet tall."

David smiled. "Six feet two inches. I am thirteen. My sister is eleven. Yes, I'm tall."

"But you're . . . like me, right?" Jonah said it cautiously, although he wasn't sure why.

"If you mean, I am part angel, a quarterling—yes," he answered. "Some of my height has come from this special gift. You're not short yourself."

"I used to be," Jonah said, pushing himself back so that he rested against the wall. "But once I discovered my abilities, it was weird. I started growing taller . . . faster."

His Ugandan roommate nodded thoughtfully. "It is the gift of Elohim. He knew who we were before we were born. He knows how tall we are going to grow and what our powers are. What our futures hold. And He knew that we were going to be put together as roommates today."

David nodded to himself, with his eyes closed for a minute.

Jonah watched him and had to admit that he enjoyed hearing David talk about Elohim. There was something in his voice that made it sound so . . . real.

"So your mother," Jonah said. "Where is she now? And your father?"

David's face grew dim for the first time, and he looked down to the floor and began to pull at a piece of rubber on his old sneaker. "It is only by the will of Elohim that my sister and I are even here. That anyone is still alive. Our house caught fire last night. Rather, it was set on fire. Our guardian angel was nowhere to be found. Thankfully, my sister smelled the smoke. We got out just in time."

He pulled the piece of rubber off his shoe and threw it toward the wastebasket in the corner.

"They have moved my father and mother to a safe location. I am not even sure where it is, but likely somewhere out of our country, where they can be hidden and watched over carefully. Abaddon is still after the nephilim and their children."

Jonah nodded. "Yeah, we had some run-ins with them ourselves."

He recounted the story of the attacks yesterday at their school and then on the way to the convent and how they barely survived.

"So now your school thinks you tried to flood it, huh?" David asked, disbelief in his voice.

"Yeah, pretty much."

David started laughing, softly at first, covering his mouth. But his laugh erupted loudly, and he began to lean back on his bed, a deep uncontrollable laugh. "Jonah Stone is a . . . how do you say it in America . . . a gangster?" He hooted even louder.

"You think that's funny? How is getting accused of flooding

my school funny?" asked Jonah. But he began to chuckle a little bit too. "Okay, it is kind of funny, in a twisted sort of way."

Jonah checked his watch.

"It will be ten thirty soon," he said.

David untied his small stack of books and grabbed one of them. It looked to Jonah like a weathered Bible.

The tall Ugandan ducked under the door frame again, and Jonah followed him, heading downstairs to the meeting room.

Jonah and David walked into the gathering room on the first floor of the convent. Someone had set up rusty folding chairs in rows, and about half of them were occupied by kids. Jonah saw Eliza, sitting in the front row, of course. She turned back and gave him a little wave. She was sitting beside a girl with jet-black hair pulled back in a ponytail. The girl turned toward him, and then looked back ahead quickly, whispering something to Eliza.

Jonah and his new roommate found two chairs in the back. Every one of the other kids sitting in the chairs turned around, almost in unison. All looking at Jonah. No one said anything to him, but a few smiled or whispered to the kids sitting beside them.

He squirmed in his seat, which made the chair creak. He met their eyes for a second, and then stared down at his worn basketball shoes. Why were they all looking at him?

Someone noisily sat down beside him.

"Hey, Jonah!" Jeremiah's voice echoed in the room, but he didn't seem to notice. "What's this all about? Do you know what we're doing here? Who's this? Have you met my roommate yet?"

Some of the girls turned toward Jeremiah and smiled. He just kept on talking. Clueless.

"Can you slow down for a sec?" Jonah said.

"This is your brother?" David said, pointing his thumb to

Jeremiah. Jonah nodded reluctantly, and David extended his huge hand toward him. "Hi, Jeremiah. My name is David."

Jeremiah took his hand and shook it forcefully, his bright eyes beaming at David.

"You're big!" he said. "How tall are you? Do you play basketball?"

David laughed. "Your brother is trouble, Jonah. I can already tell."

Before he could answer the barrage of questions, Sister Patricia had moved to the front of the room. The remaining chairs filled up with kids.

"Good afternoon, children," she said kindly. "I want to welcome you all again to our convent. I hope that you have found your rooms adequate."

None of the kids said anything, and Jonah wondered if they were thinking the same thing he was. He was already missing his room and his stuff.

"As you know, you have been brought here by the angelic forces. This has been done for your protection. Most of the missing guardian angels have been recovered. They have taken your parents to safe places near your homelands, guarded securely, hidden from Abaddon and his forces." She paced in front of them as she spoke. "And you have been brought here for you own safety." The kids nodded solemnly. Jonah counted them. Thirteen quarterlings, all attacked and driven from their homes the day before.

"But there is another reason you are here." She paused, and then her eyes landed past them, to the back of the room.

"Training."

The voice came from behind Jonah and was a familiar one. He turned to see an elderly woman standing in the doorway. She was wearing a blue dress with a shawl wrapped around her shoulders and had a cane in her hand. Slowly, she crept toward the front of the room, as all of the kids looked on. A few whispered to each other.

Jonah found himself smiling. It was his old friend Camilla Aldridge. They never would have rescued the nephilim without her help.

"Excuse me, but what can you possibly tell us about training?"

The question came from a boy sitting at the end of Jonah's row. He leaned back in his chair, arms folded, a smirk on his face. His sandy blond hair fell over his forehead, his skin tanned and golden.

Jonah narrowed his eyes at him. "More than you ever could."

The kid leaned forward, looking for who had said those words. When he realized it was Jonah, for a second he looked uncertain. But his glare quickly turned icy. Jonah met it with a sarcastic wave. He noticed the other kids watching him, and his face began to feel flushed. Thankfully, Mrs. Aldridge drew their attention back to the front of the room.

"Things aren't always what they seem, Frederick," she said with a smile. As she stood in front of them, she suddenly began to transform. Her hunched-over back straightened and her wrinkles disappeared, her face taking on an otherworldly glow. Her hair lengthened, turning from grayish-blue to brilliant silver. Wings of the same color emerged from her back, fluttering softly. Her blue dress morphed into a long, flowing robe that sparkled as if it were covered with diamonds. The cane she had been holding became a glittering sword, which she sheathed inside her robe.

The kids oohed and aahed, and even Frederick seemed reluctantly impressed. Jonah wondered if they had ever seen warrior angels before their journey here.

"Ah, yes. That feels better," she said, stretching her arms

and twisting her back. "It's rather like wearing a fat suit. Very constricting."

Some of the kids laughed. She measured them all for a minute with her blue eyes. *Her eyes are still the same*, Jonah thought to himself.

"Now, as Sister Patricia has told you, being here is for your own protection. Your guardian angels are not here to protect you any longer. You might have noticed that they disappeared yesterday. They were kidnapped by Abaddon's forces, part of the plan to attack you."

The room grew silent once more. *So that's what happened to Cassandra*, Jonah thought.

"This place is covered with the prayers of the nuns and the wings of the angels. A very strong defense against the wiles of the fallen ones. They cannot locate us, much less penetrate these walls."

"Ex-excuse me," one of the boys said, shooting up his hand nervously. He was dressed in khaki slacks, a blue button-down shirt, and a red sweater vest. His reddish-brown hair was slicked down and neatly parted.

"Yes, Mr. Clamwater?" Camilla said patiently.

Jonah recognized the name, and when the boy began to speak, he immediately remembered. The boy's father, Roger Clamwater, was the first nephilim to fall under Marduk's spell, down underneath the psychiatric center in New York last year. He had survived, barely. This boy spoke with the same thin British accent. This must be his kid.

"How can you be sure? Wouldn't they notice all the angels on the roof? We were all told we were perfectly safe before, but nothing stopped the Fallen from attacking yesterday. My dad was caught in a drive-by shooting in broad daylight—right outside Parliament!"

he said, arms folded across his chest, rubbing his arms. His voice grew higher as he spoke. "He almost died! I'm sorry, but the angels did nothing to stop that, did they? So how can you know, I mean *really* know, that—"

"Rupert," Camilla said, just firmly enough to stop him mid-sentence. "I understand your worries, my dear. As I said, one of the reasons you are here is that this is an extremely secure location. There is not one possibility of a fallen angel breaking through our defenses. The entire Second Battalion is ready to intercede at any moment. And your parents have the protection of Elohim's angels as well."

This seemed to settle Rupert down, if only a little. He continued mumbling something but kept it to himself.

Eliza slowly raised her hand, pushing her glasses up onto her nose. "Mrs. Aldridge?" she asked.

"Yes, dear? And please, call me Camilla."

Eliza nodded. "You said that we are also here to be trained. What does that mean?"

"I can always count on you to listen well, Eliza," Camilla said. Her eyes glistened now, and she began pacing in front of them, hands folded behind her back. "It is my duty to inform you that, by the order of the Archangel Michael himself, under the hand of our Lord Elohim, a new effort is beginning as of today. A training center for quarterlings, all thirteen of you, has been established."

The kids began talking to each other rapidly, excitement suddenly filling the air of the dusty meeting room.

"This center will focus on preparing you to be the best quarterlings possible," she continued. "All of the angelic skills necessary to do battle will be learned. Archery, swordsmanship, using your unique defenses, to name a few. As well as the more focused, spiritual exercises, like prayer and studying the Scriptures—they don't get all the glory, but they are just as necessary to the battle."

Jeremiah raised his hand frantically but didn't wait for her to call on him. "Will there be recess?"

Everyone laughed, including Camilla. "There will be some time for relaxation, yes. But listen," she said, her voice growing very serious, the smile vanishing from her face for the first time. "We will not be learning simple lessons never to be used again outside a classroom. There is a battle happening, and the lives of everyone you see are at stake. But the humans . . ." She paused, sighing. "Humans are who Abaddon is really after. Elohim's prized creation. Your job will be to learn your gifts, to encourage one another, to work hard, and to fight well."

Jonah looked around at the rest of the kids, sizing up his new classmates. He wondered what kinds of skills they had already developed. And he couldn't help but think about how he would fare against them. This wasn't like math or science class. Real life was at stake, just like Camilla had said. He knew that as well as anybody. Maybe these kids weren't even all followers of Elohim. Were some of them loyal to Abaddon instead? He finally raised his hand.

"Yes, Jonah?" Camilla responded. The other kids cocked their heads around to get a glimpse of him again. They also seemed to be sizing up Eliza. He tried to ignore the stares.

"Mrs. Aldridge," he said, "this . . . um . . . angel school . . . is it going to meet here? I mean, just looking around this place, it doesn't seem like there is any space for this kind of thing."

"*Angel School* . . . Well put, Jonah," she replied, looking thoughtfully at him for a minute. "To keep current with your regular schooling, the nuns have agreed to tutor you here in the convent."

All of the quarterlings groaned at the same time. Camilla waited until they were quiet again.

"We, however, have arranged a different space for our lessons. Since there are only thirteen of you, you will all be taught together. We have some very gifted teachers who will be instructing you. I can't wait for you to meet them."

Rupert raised his hand tentatively again. He looked like he was going to be sick. "So this begins now, then?"

Camilla snapped her fingers. "I'm glad you brought that up, Rupert! Actually, it begins tonight."

A buzz swept through the kids again. School at *night*?

"Now, enough questions for today," she said. "A special brunch has been prepared for you by the sisters of the convent. I hope you will use the day as a time to rest and get to know one another. You'll start your regular classes tomorrow. But we will meet back here tonight at nine o'clock, for the beginning of Angel School . . . Yes, we'll call it that." She glanced at Jonah and smiled. "You will get more answers to your questions tonight, I am sure."

With that, she flapped her wings ever so slightly and hovered toward the back of the room—whether she was walking or floating Jonah couldn't tell—and disappeared through the open door.

NINE

CLASS BEGINS

Camilla Aldridge was waiting in the meeting room when Jonah, Eliza, and Jeremiah arrived at nine o'clock. A few of the quarterlings were there, and the others trickled through the door.

"Hurry along, students," she said. "You cannot be late to our session—you will miss class. And there is much to see tonight."

Frederick stood right beside Camilla, listening attentively. Jonah caught his eye briefly, and Frederick glared at him. Jonah wasn't sure why the other boy seemed to hate him so much, but he knew he should try to rise above it. Jonah quickly looked away, shoving his hands in his pockets. He tried to focus his attention on their new leader.

Camilla was wearing the same blue, shiny robe, and she spoke both with an authority and enthusiasm that drew all of their eyes.

"Before we do anything, we shall ask for Elohim's blessing," she said. "Let's pray together." All of the students bowed their heads. Camilla raised her hands in the air.

"Father Elohim, we are blessed by Your presence tonight. Lead us together. Help us learn about one another—and about You. Give us the strength to fight the good fight of faith. Protect these children and their parents. Thank You for the gift of hospitality from our sisters here. In Your Son's precious name, amen."

Jonah and the rest repeated *amen* quietly.

"Okay then," Camilla said, clapping her hands together loudly. "The best way to get to where we are going is by entering into the hidden realm. Now, is there anyone here who has not done this before?"

A handful of kids raised their hands, including Frederick.

"Your first lesson, then," she said, smiling. "Nothing to worry about. It is as easy as breathing. After a little practice, it will become second nature to each of you."

Jonah nodded. He remembered the first time he had entered the hidden realm, this spiritual world that was a layer behind the physical world—the place where the battle between the angels can be seen—and how amazed he was at what he saw.

"Since each of you has angel blood coursing through your veins, it is within each of your abilities to come and go in the hidden realm as you wish. All you need to do, children, is pray, and believe that it exists."

She looked at each of their faces. "Ready, everyone?"

They nodded. Jeremiah reached out and grabbed Jonah's hand. Even though he had entered the hidden realm with Jonah the day before, it was still new to him. Jonah could see a hint of nervousness on his brother's face.

"Very well," she said. "Bow your heads with me, and in your heart, say something like this: 'Dear Elohim, I believe not only in the physical world but in the spiritual things that cannot always be seen—the hidden realm. Allow me passage into this place now.'"

As they prayed, Jonah opened one eye, peeking in time to see each of the quarterlings, one at a time, begin to disappear. *Pop, pop, pop.* They were here one minute and gone the next. Just before he slipped into the spiritual world, he glanced down at Jeremiah and saw him disappear too.

Closing his eyes, he felt something inside him shift, and he knew that when he opened his eyes again, he would see all of the students there with him in the room.

When he looked up, Camilla was standing in front of them, just as she had been. Everyone was in the same place. Jeremiah was still holding his hand, squeezing it a little tighter.

"Cool!" Jeremiah said, looking at Jonah. He looked the same, except that a glowing light emanated from the center of his chest, stretching its fingers out to his arms.

Jeremiah turned and beamed at Eliza, who had the same glow, and then at his own light-filled chest.

Jonah looked around at the rest of the quarterlings. Entering this world always amazed him, no matter how many times he did it. There was a glow that every person had—the thumbprint of Elohim, the Creator of everyone. But some had a brighter, more profound glow. And he couldn't help but notice that some of the quarterlings did not.

Camilla quickly addressed this before anyone could point out the obvious. "In the hidden realm, we see the glow of Elohim within every living person—every living thing, for that matter." Jonah remembered how he could see the grass and trees sparkle from Elohim's touch. "It is also possible to see the bright glow of those who have invited Elohim into their lives and have accepted His forgiveness through His Son."

Some of the quarterlings—Hai Ling, a girl form China; Lania, an Australian; Rupert, the English boy; and Frederick— had very dull glows. Sensing the eyes of the others, each of them took either an awkward step backward or began to stare down at the floor. Except for Frederick, who stood with his eyes locked straight ahead, not moving an inch.

"A word of warning, and perhaps encouragement, to you all," said Camilla, gathering their attention back to herself. "Do not judge those who have not yet called upon Elohim. He can use all of us in mighty ways, if He wills. And do not, under any circum- stances, allow yourselves to separate out those without the glow from those with it. There is plenty of time for Elohim to work and draw hearts to Himself."

∽

If anyone had been standing outside the convent on the dark street, watching, they would have sworn that the door opened all by itself. In reality, thirteen quarterlings and one warrior angel opened it and walked out onto the New York City sidewalk. The quarterlings stayed close together, trying to keep up with Camilla, who was moving with purpose.

In the hidden realm, they couldn't be seen or heard. But the only time Camilla spoke, or even stopped, was when she came across a man sprawled out on the ground, asleep on a vent in the concrete. She halted abruptly when she spotted him, bent down, and cradled his dirty face in her hands. Jonah watched as she bent down and kissed his forehead. The man turned his head up, opened his eyes for a second, then closed them again and returned to sleep.

"Bless you, my brother," she said softly. "Elohim loves you deeply."

Jonah saw the man smile and mutter something. Camilla held his face for a few more seconds, and then stood. Jonah silently wondered if he would have even noticed the man if she hadn't stopped.

"Ah," she said, almost as if she'd forgotten they were there. "Let's keep going, shall we? Almost there."

Their curiosity for where "there" was grew by the second. The quarterlings started whispering back and forth to each other.

"I think she's crazy," Jonah overheard Frederick say. "Why is she taking us out here in the dark? The streets of New York are the safest place for us to be? Really?"

"Oh, just trust her, okay?" Eliza shot back at him, looking disgusted. "I'm pretty sure she knows where she's going."

Finally, Camilla stopped in front of a set of white granite steps that led up to a large building with tall columns across the front.

"Here we are, students," Camilla said.

Jonah looked at the sign by the street. It read:

New York Public Library
Hours: 9:00 a.m.–9:00 p.m. Daily

He raised his hand slowly. "We're going to have classes . . . at the library?"

"That's right," she said. "We'll be using the side entrance, though. Even though they are closed, we don't want to draw too much attention to ourselves now, do we?"

Before anyone else could ask a question, she headed down a path that led to the side of the building. There was a single door there. Rupert went ahead of her and tugged on the handle.

"It's open," he said, turning the handle and pushing the door open slightly.

"Of course it is, dear," she said with a sly smile. "We have friends in high places."

"Right this way," Camilla called out as she walked through the door. "Follow me. Quickly now."

Jonah gazed up at the ceiling and the walls as they walked quietly through the hallway. It was the largest library he had ever seen. Everything seemed made out of marble, and large paintings of serious-looking people hung on the walls. The library in Peacefield was a small, one-floor building with old, tacky carpet and only a few shelves in the youth section.

They rounded the corner and saw that Camilla had stopped. Standing with her hand up in the air, she motioned for them to move over against the wall.

A security guard was coming down the stone steps with a security dog on a leash, clicking his flashlight against the railing and whistling a tune. They all sucked in a breath of air and held it, even though they all knew he couldn't see or hear them.

In nervous silence they watched as he ambled down the hallway. He stopped to get a long drink of water at the fountain. Just as Jonah and the rest were breathing a sigh of relief, the German shepherd turned its head toward them and barked once. Its eyes narrowed as it seemed to look right at Jonah.

The dog pulled the guard over until they were right in front of Jonah. It began to sniff around excitedly at Jonah's feet and barked again several times.

Jonah tried not to breathe as he looked down at the dog in front of him. His mind told him it couldn't bite him in the hidden realm. But everything in him wanted to run.

"What's gotten into you, Molly?" the guard said, looking down at his dog strangely. "There's nothing here. Just an empty hallway."

He tugged at her leash, pulling her down the hall after him. The dog continued to look backward but followed her master's orders.

"That's why we always stay in the hidden realm when we are here," Camilla said after they had turned the corner.

She continued up a flight of stairs until they arrived in front of a sign that said MAIN READING ROOM.

"Here we are!" she announced, beaming back at the kids.

"How is it possible," Eliza asked, keeping her voice barely above a whisper, "that we are having class in the New York Public Library? It just doesn't seem like it would be, well . . . allowed." She pushed her glasses up on her nose and looked at Camilla.

"As I said, we have friends in high places, dear," she said with a twinkle in her eye and a mysterious tone in her voice. "The director of the New York Public Libraries is sympathetic to our cause."

They walked into the largest reading room Jonah had ever seen. There were thousands of books lining every wall from floor to ceiling. Dozens of wooden tables sat in perfect symmetry on the floor, bronze reading lamps and computer docking stations on each one.

"This must be the size of two football fields," Jonah said to David.

David was in awe. "I've never seen so many books in one place before. You could stay in this one room for the rest of your life and never run out of interesting things to read." Out of the corner of his eye, Jonah saw Eliza give an approving nod.

Some of the kids were looking up at the ceiling. Jonah's eyes were drawn there too, to the sky blue images painted across it.

"It's like we're outside under a sunny blue sky," Jeremiah said.

Camilla let them take in the room for a few minutes.

"Okay, enough gazing at the walls, students," she finally said, standing in the center of the room. "You can come have a seat at these tables."

After they had been seated, she continued, "We thought this would be the ideal setting to begin our studies together. Here we will hone our skills. Your minds will be sharpened, your gifts will be stretched and encouraged, and if you give yourself fully to the process of learning, you will become a better quarterling and a better servant of Elohim."

She paced around the tables as she spoke, hands behind her back.

"Angel School has begun," she announced. "And for our first order of business, I would like to introduce you to your instructors."

TEN

THE GIFTINGS

Immediately, three people walked through a doorway across the room and marched toward the students. They quietly stood in front of them in a line.

"Marcus and Taryn!" Eliza whispered to Jonah, pointing to the large, muscular angel standing on the end and the angel beside him with the brilliant shock of red hair.

Jonah nodded. Next to them stood another angel, holding a large, dusty book at his side. He didn't appear to Jonah to be a warrior angel. He was a couple of heads shorter than Marcus, and slight and thin. He had dark brown skin and a rather skinny neck, which made his gray robe appear to be too large on him.

Camilla stood beside the three angels. "Our classes will be divided into three categories—Angelic Combat, Scriptural Studies, and the Spiritual Arts. Marcus and Taryn will be teaching Angelic Combat." Some of the boys nudged one another and smiled. "They are warrior class angels of the highest caliber.

You will learn how to use the gifts you've been given to fight and defend yourself. You will find none better than they to provide you with this instruction." The angels bowed their heads slightly as she walked in front of them.

"Your Scriptural Studies instructor will be Samuel." The third angel nodded thoughtfully at the students. "There is no finer scholar of the Scriptures than he. From him your knowledge of the Bible will be sharpened, and he will help you discover its endless treasures, as well as its uses in the battle against the dark forces."

Some of the quarterlings, including Frederick, looked less excited about this. But Jonah was curious. His knowledge of the Bible was not the best, and he wondered how he would fare in this class. Eliza nodded along enthusiastically, of course.

"And there is one more instructor who will be joining us," Camilla said. "I should let you know that he is human."

Jonah and Eliza glanced at one another. How was that supposed to work?

"You will meet him before the night is over. We didn't feel it prudent or safe for him to be here right now, considering his inability to enter the hidden realm. Plus"—she laughed—"he wouldn't be able to see you right now, would he? You will have to emerge from the realm for his class. His name is Reverend Bashir, and he is deeply gifted in this subject. He will be teaching the Spiritual Arts."

Jeremiah looked at the others and slowly raised his hand. "I had language arts in school last year. Is it kind of like that?"

"Actually, Jeremiah, spiritual arts do involve language arts in a way. They are the often-overlooked weapons in the battle," Camilla replied. "It is another realm of knowledge and practice. More subtle, yes, but just as effective. Prayer, scriptural meditation, fasting, to name a few. There are many ways humans can enter the battle. And since you are mostly human," she said, looking each quarterling in the eye, "it is important you learn the spiritual arts.

"Now," Camilla continued, clasping her hands together. "On to the task of grouping you."

She pulled out a huge leather-bound book with a golden clasp and placed it on the table in the center of the room. In her hand she held a key, which she inserted into a small hole, then turned. The book opened itself.

"Ladies first," she announced. "Eliza, step forward."

Eliza adjusted her glasses and moved toward the table, watching Camilla for further instruction.

The angel pointed her finger to a passage. Jonah saw Eliza smile slightly, as if she recognized it, and she began to read.

"'Therefore put on the full armor of God, so that when the day of evil comes, you may be able to stand your ground, and after you have done everything, to stand. Stand firm then, with the belt of truth buckled around your waist, with the breastplate of righteousness in place, and with your feet fitted with the readiness that comes from the gospel of peace. In addition to all this, take up the shield of faith, with which you can extinguish all the flaming arrows of the evil one. Take the helmet of salvation and the sword of the Spirit, which is the word of God.'"

Then Camilla pointed her to a passage from the book of Romans about spiritual gifts.

When Eliza looked up, Jonah could see Camilla lock eyes with his sister. The angel was looking for something, and Jonah couldn't help but think that she was actually searching behind Eliza's eyes.

Then the angel began to pray, but in a foreign language. Jonah somehow knew immediately that she was speaking in the angelic tongue. The beautiful, mysterious words rolled from her mouth as she continued to search.

When she was finally finished, she nodded, smiled at Eliza, said, "Very interesting," and made notes in another smaller book made of the same worn leather.

Eliza seemed to shake herself from the daze she was in, and then turned to rejoin the others, rubbing her eye with the palm of her hand.

One by one Camilla called the girls up and had them read the passages, and then she prayed, again peering at each one closely. The boys followed. Jonah read the same words aloud and tried to peek at her notebook, but all he saw were scribbles on the page.

She stared at him longer than the others, with a mysterious gaze that Jonah couldn't decipher. A flash of darkness came across the deep blue orbs gazing at him, and a chill shuddered along his spine.

She said nothing, but finally began to scribble furiously in her notebook.

"What did you see?" he asked, eyeing her book. But she didn't speak to him, or even look up, as she continued to write. Instead, she addressed all of the quarterlings.

"You have all just participated in a gift grouping: a way for Elohim to reveal to me the gifts He has given to you. That way, we can place you in the appropriate group."

Rupert waved his hand in the air. "Well, what are the gifts, then? I for one would like to know." Some of the other kids nodded their heads as well.

"Patience, dear Rupert." She smiled. "Elohim reveals your

gifts to you when He deems necessary. It is not for the angels to reveal all of His purposes."

Camilla looked at her notes and began splitting the kids up according to what she'd written. The first group went with Samuel down to the other side of the reading room. They sat at a table in the corner. It was so far away that Jonah couldn't have heard them if he'd wanted to.

The second group went with Camilla out of the room and into a hallway. Apparently there was another classroom where the Spiritual Arts would be taught.

Jonah, Eliza, and Jeremiah were all in different groups. Frederick was selected to join Jonah's group. *Just my luck*, Jonah thought. Also joining Jonah was his roommate, David, Lania from Australia, and Hai Ling, the Chinese quarterling who still looked less than thrilled to be there. Jonah tried to quickly analyze the groups. They must be grouped together by gifts . . . but what were those gifts, exactly?

Marcus and Taryn began pushing tables against the walls of the reading room. A rectangular space was cleared out in the middle. Jonah figured it was as wide—and almost as long—as the basketball court in their school gym back in Peacefield. At one end, they positioned two tables up on their sides. Marcus pulled two pieces of paper out from his belt. He unfolded two bull's-eye images and tacked them onto each of the table bottoms.

"This is no ordinary paper," he said as the quarterlings watched him. "When your arrow hits this, it will stick, not just dissolve away."

Taryn nodded. "This will be our combat practice area every time we are together. Elohim has made it clear to us that you need to be able to protect yourself, so the first gift many of you will discover is a weapon to be used in combat. One of the gifts you all share is angelic archery. Some of you have experience with this." She gave Jonah a knowing smile. Frederick noticed this and rolled his eyes. "Have any of the rest of you had any archery practice?"

Frederick and Lania raised their hands.

"Marcus, why don't you take those three? I'll work with our beginners, David and Hai Ling."

She took David and Hai Ling over to the side and began to instruct them on how to pull out an arrow. David was eager, but Hai Ling stood listening with her arms folded. At Taryn's insistence, she finally reached back over her shoulder and pulled out a white flaming arrow. She looked at it, seeming almost surprised that she could actually pull an angel arrow out of thin air and hold it in her hand. Before she knew it, a bow had appeared in her left hand.

Marcus stood with Jonah and Frederick. "All right, let's see what you boys have."

Frederick stepped up. "Let me go first," he said, and abruptly pulled an arrow off his back. He grinned as his bow appeared in his other hand. "Cool!"

"Very well," Marcus said, motioning him forward with his arm. "We will start here." He pointed down to a line in the floor formed by a crack.

Frederick stood at the mark, pulled his arrow back, and fired.

The arrow pierced the red center of the bull's-eye on the paper and stuck there. He smiled smugly, glancing back at Jonah.

"Excellent!" Marcus said, clearly impressed. "You've had some practice."

Frederick nodded. "It's no big deal. We bow hunt at my parents' compound all the time."

"Jonah?" said Marcus. "Why don't you give it a go?"

Jonah doubted Frederick had more experience, at least at shooting angel arrows, than he did. Confidently, he pulled an arrow off his back and put his toe up beside the mark. The bow appeared in his left hand, and he took aim and fired.

The arrow flew wildly off to the left, careening into a bookshelf and disintegrating.

"Hmm," said Marcus. "Try to focus a little more on the target, Jonah."

Jonah didn't turn around, but he could hear Frederick snickering behind him. He quickly pulled another arrow and fired. It only ended up a little better this time, hitting the top right corner of the target.

"Better," said the angel. "But you clearly need more practice." And he began to instruct Jonah in the finer points of holding a bow, how to aim, and releasing it at the proper time. He was full of advice and instruction, and while Jonah tried to listen and take it in, he could feel Frederick behind him. *Probably still laughing*, he thought. He had more experience fighting fallen angels than all of the other quarterlings combined—except Eliza, of course—yet here he was, getting a basic lesson on how to hold a bow and shoot an arrow.

What made it worse was that when it was Lania's turn, she strode up and fired her arrow right into the red center of the bull's-eye too. She shrugged and said nothing.

"Nice work, Lania," said Marcus. "Looks like you're a natural."

She blushed, looking down at her sneakers. "Thanks."

For the next hour, they practiced. Frederick continued to either hit or come close to the bull's-eye at every turn, earning the admiration of Marcus. Lania was not quite as accurate, but almost. Jonah was turning out to be the worst. He wondered where the touch he seemed to have last year, in the real battle, had gone. He struggled to even hit the target, finding the wall three more times.

Exasperated, he was glad when, mercifully, Camilla announced that it was time to switch classes.

"I'm sure you'll do better next time, Stone," Frederick said, patting him hard on the shoulder. Jonah quickly pushed his arm off and sighed loudly. Maybe this was not going to be as easy as he thought.

✿

Staring at this big book in front of him in Samuel's class, Jonah couldn't help but feel a little intimidated. *This class might not be so easy either.*

"Jonah Stone." Samuel said his name loudly, nodding in approval of his new student. Jonah looked up from the table and raised his eyebrow. "It is a real pleasure to have you and your family with us."

Jonah wasn't sure what he was supposed to say. "Thanks," he muttered, eager to get the spotlight off himself after his dismal failure in Angelic Combat. But Samuel continued on.

"Your sister, Eliza, was a pleasure," he said, almost gushing. "Her knowledge of the Scriptures, for someone her age, is quite extraordinary. I hope that I will find the same is true of you." Jonah tried to smile and look at him confidently, but accidentally made a noise that sounded like a wince. "You and your sister have made tremendous progress, tremendous progress . . ."

Jonah could feel the stares of the others on him, but he didn't dare look over at them. He was sure Frederick would have something to say. The last thing he needed was special treatment from one of their instructors. That was more trouble than it was worth.

"So, ah . . . what are we going to learn today?" Jonah said, although as soon as the words left his lips, he wished they hadn't. In trying to get the attention off himself, it made him sound like he was returning the compliments with some sucking up of his own.

Samuel beamed. "Yes, yes, of course! Now where to begin . . ." He began thumbing through the giant Bible in front of him, dust flying off it.

"Ah, yes," he said, "an overview is in order."

For the next hour, he proceeded to walk them through the entire Bible, talking with more enthusiasm than Jonah would have expected from looking at the angel. He began in Genesis— actually, before Genesis—talking about the existence of Elohim as God Three-in-One.

"We'll come back to that," he said with excitement, a phrase that Jonah and the students would hear often from him. He mentioned the creation of the angels.

"We'll come back to that."

And then he spoke about the angelic rebellion, a brief shadow tarnishing his glow for a moment.

"And, of course, we'll come back to that too."

He moved through the Old Testament in a flash, and Jonah found it hard to stay with him. Each of the kids had a notebook and pencil in front of them, and Jonah tried to write down as much as he could, but it was no use. Samuel blazed through the Old Testament law, the judges, and then the prophets.

"Who can tell me about the prophet Malachi?" he asked,

searching the faces of the five students in front of him, which had just gone blank. "Jonah?"

He waited for an intelligent response from Jonah, but when Jonah heard his name called out, his mind ground to a halt.

"Uhh . . ." was all Jonah could muster. Samuel looked terribly disappointed, but brightened when David spoke up.

"Malachi was one of the minor prophets, around the same time as Nehemiah," said David. "'But unto you that fear my name shall the Sun of righteousness arise with healing in his wings.' Malachi 4:2."

Samuel beamed. "Very nice, David. Very nice indeed."

He spent a lot of time, and his most passionate comments, on the birth and life of Jesus in the Gospels. And when he came to the death and resurrection, his voice grew low, to barely a whisper. The students, even Frederick, Jonah noticed, were leaning forward, listening intently. Samuel spoke of the events almost as if he had actually been there, not merely as some old, out-of-touch professor talking about the history of long ago.

He paused to catch his breath, and for their final twenty minutes launched into his comments on the book of Acts, about the very first group of believers, then the letters of Paul, and finally the book of Revelation.

He looked at his watch. "But we'll come back to that," he said, once more.

Finally, Samuel closed his Bible and stepped back, clearly having exhausted himself, as well as the students.

"Wow," David said as they stood up from the table. "That hour went by very quickly, don't you think?"

Jonah nodded. "I never thought the Bible would be so . . ."

"Interesting?" said David, grinning.

"Well, yeah, interesting," Jonah said.

Jonah looked at his watch. 12:03. He stretched his arms out, feeling himself growing tired. He saw the looks on the faces of the other students too. It had been a long day, and it wasn't over yet. He wondered how they were going to handle late-night sessions.

"You will get used to the timing of these classes," said Camilla as they passed by, as if reading his thoughts. "Besides, you'll get to sleep in each morning. Just what you've always wanted in a school, right? The chance to sleep late!"

She chuckled to herself and walked over to another group, trying to keep tabs on all of the students at once. She informed them that after their final class, they would gather back together for a time with her. Time to talk through their experiences together, share what they had learned, and hear directly from Camilla.

Jonah watched as Eliza's group emerged from a door in the hallway across the room and tried to read the looks on their faces. They spoke together in hushed tones as they walked over toward Marcus and Taryn's area. Before they did, they stopped to pray silently. He saw the glimmer return in each of them, and he knew they'd entered the hidden realm again.

"Well," Jonah said, punching David in the arm. "Time to meet the mystery teacher face-to-face."

ELEVEN

THE SPIRITUAL ARTS

Jonah and his classmates stood in the hallway in front of the closed wooden door. They looked at each other, suddenly aware that leaving the hidden realm meant that any human who might accidentally walk into the hall would be able to see them.

"What's this class going to be?" asked Frederick. "Listening to some old guy ramble again, like the last one?"

He laughed, but no one else laughed along with him. Jonah was determined to take the high road and try to ignore him.

"I guess it's time to come back into sight," Jonah said. He bowed his head and quieted himself, offering a sincere prayer out loud so the others would also know what to say. He felt the change, and when he opened his eyes, he knew he was back.

The other kids followed his lead, and when they were ready, Jonah opened the door and entered the room.

The soft glow of candlelight flickered against the beige walls. It was a small space but cozy. Tall candles were lit and had been positioned along the walls. Instead of a table in the room, there was a circle of chairs, six in all.

"Welcome, friends," a man said softly, standing in the middle of the room. He motioned to the chairs around him. "Please take a seat."

Jonah and the others stared at him for a few seconds. He wore a black T-shirt, and his hands were slid comfortably into the pockets of his dark jeans. His hair was as black as his shirt, and it swept across his forehead and down almost to his shoulders. A goatee covered his chin. Tattoos covered the brown skin on his left arm down to his wrist. Lania and Hai Ling hadn't blinked at all and seemed suddenly taken with the new instructor.

He sized them up with warm brown eyes and an easy smile. The quarterlings quietly found a seat. A silver cross hung around his neck, drawing Jonah's eyes. The candlelight glistened against it, causing it to shift from silver to crimson red and back again.

"My name is Reverend Kareem Bashir," the man said. "Please, call me Kareem."

As he spoke, his bright eyes shone, and he bore them into each of the kids intently, as if searching for something beneath their skin. Jonah met his piercing gaze for a few seconds. Soon, though, he found himself glancing away uncomfortably.

"I live here in New York, where I pastor a church my wife and I began seven years ago," he said. "But as you may be able to tell from my accent, I'm not from here originally. I am Pakistani by birth. In fact, most of my family still lives there."

David raised his hand. "How did you get here, then?"

Kareem folded his arms, his smile turning into an easy laugh. "It's a long and crazy story that perhaps I'll tell you sometime. My family is Muslim, but I was able to come to college in the States.

I found Jesus—or rather, He found me—one night through a conversation with a friend in my college dorm room. That night I became a Christ-follower. Not long after that, I was called to start a new church in this amazing city.

"I'm friends with Sister Patricia," he continued, "and she told me about you extraordinary kids and requested that I come. I sensed that Elohim was moving mightily here. How could I refuse? My job is to help you learn how to practice what are called the Spiritual Arts: those practices, the disciplines of the spirit, that can lead a person to a deeper communion with Elohim."

Jonah glanced over at Frederick. In spite of their new instructor, he already looked bored. Kareem was acting as if he didn't notice, but Jonah wasn't so sure.

"I'm sorry," Frederick blurted out, "but what can someone like you possibly teach us about prayer and this other stuff?" He seemed to be staring at Kareem's tattoos.

Kareem glanced down at his arm but continued smiling. "There are no experts in the spiritual arts, my friend. Just learners. We will learn together. I will say, however, that I do have some experience that will be helpful to you. I began our church with only prayer, after all."

"What is it up to now?" scoffed Frederick. "A dozen people or so?"

Kareem pushed his fingers through his hair as he thought. "I think around three thousand. Now, shall we get started?"

Frederick snapped his mouth shut, and the others nodded.

"Now, you all look human to me," Kareem said, causing Hai Ling and Lania to giggle. He sat down with them and began to speak a little lower. "Of course, I know your true identities. That each of you is part angel, offspring of both human and nephilim.

You are amazing kids, with much to offer this world. Just like all of Elohim's children. I've heard that some of you have already been using your gifts quite effectively."

He glanced at Jonah and nodded. Jonah blushed, and Kareem seemed to get the hint and moved on quickly.

"I must confess I've never been around quarterlings before. It's a pretty cool experience for someone like me. But just like the rest of us," he said, "prayer is the central connection we have to Elohim. You will never realize your full potential to engage in the battle between good and evil if you can't, or won't, pray. So why don't you join me now?"

He reached out and extended his hands to the right and left, grabbing the hands of Frederick and David. Frederick looked as if he was going to pull away but didn't. Jonah, Lania, and Hai Ling followed suit, each reaching out to hold hands with the kids next to them.

"Close your eyes, friends," he said, and they obediently followed his direction. "This will allow you the least amount of distraction. Let everything that is worrying you, all of your cares, all of your fears, your doubts . . . let it all blow away, like a dandelion in the breeze. Now, turn your mind to Elohim, think about Him, invite Him to come into view, and ask Him what He wants to say . . ."

Kareem kept speaking softly, not so much praying as encouraging the students to pray themselves. Jonah kept his eyes closed, trying to concentrate. But his mind kept wandering off in a thousand directions. His parents, the flood in the school bathroom, his house and all the things he wished he'd brought from his room—when he tried to concentrate on Elohim, all of these random thoughts kept interrupting.

He took a deep breath. *Let those things go, Jonah . . . let them blow away.* He pictured each of his worries blowing away like one of the dandelions in his backyard, caught up in an autumn breeze.

Suddenly, Jonah sensed that something had changed.

Thud, thud, thud. Thud, thud, thud.

What is that noise? It sounded vaguely familiar. And then he heard a faint roar that grew steadily louder.

He opened his eyes again. The room around him, along with the rest of the quarterlings, had vanished. Jonah found himself standing in the center of the Granger Community School basketball court.

Thud, thud, thud.

The thudding noise was the basketball he was dribbling. The growing roar now filled up his ears. He looked up, and on both sides of the court, bleachers full of fans were screaming. He found himself momentarily captivated by their faces. Because even though they were looking at him, they weren't cheering. Some of them were weeping uncontrollably. Others wailed from pain, or grief. All around him were faces of human suffering.

Why are these people at a basketball game?

Quickly, though, his attention was drawn back to the court. There was a boy guarding him, and other kids running around on the court, calling to him. His teammates were yelling frantically, urging him to move the ball down the court.

He looked at the player crouched in front of him, a boy who looked about his age. He could have been any kid at Jonah's school ... except that his eyes flashed yellow. He quickly glanced at the other four kids on the opposing team. They were moving around the court, but in each of them, he saw those same yellow eyes.

Out of instinct, he glanced up at the game clock, and just as he did, he heard the voice. It was barely a whisper, and yet it somehow carried over the screams coming from the stands.

"Help . . ."

Jonah looked to his right and left, still dribbling the basketball, but saw no one nearby who could have whispered to him.

And then he realized why his teammates were yelling at him. The score read 59–58, visitors ahead. They were losing, and the clock had just crossed the ten-second mark.

:09

:08

Jonah began to move toward the basket. He needed to score. His team was down. The other team was made up of fallen angels, for some strange reason. But he couldn't shake the whisper for help out of his head.

"Help me . . ."

There it was again. The voice sounded both powerful and frail. He was distracted. More time ticked off the clock.

:07

:06

:05

He was overwhelmed by the scene. But somehow, in the middle of it, he knew that he had to try to make the basket. He knew that if he did, he just might reach the voice crying for help.

Jonah moved to the left, maneuvering around a reaching defender. He split between two more, and with a nifty through-the-legs dribble, he was open, just inside the three-point line.

:04

:03

He was about to shoot, but a hulking kid stepped up, blocking his path to the basket. He dribbled to the left but was cut off. Back to the right, but another defender had walled him in.

:02

:01

He flung it. A desperation heave over the top of the big kid's outstretched fingers. The buzzer sounded as the ball floated through the air. The arc looked good. For a second, Jonah thought he had made it.

Air ball. It missed everything.

The other team snarled and jeered at him, celebrating their victory. The crowd seemed to grow louder, their screams that much more intense. Jonah felt as though he had let them down.

Then a weird thing happened. For the briefest second, a word flickered on the scoreboard, in pink neon.

TEMPLE

Then it faded away, as quickly as it had come.

"Jonah. Jonah . . ." Above the noise of the crowd, he heard his name being called out. Was it the voice again? He looked around, trying to see who was calling him.

"Jonah!"

The sound of Kareem's voice caused his eyelids to jerk open. He was breathing heavily, sweat pouring off his forehead.

"Jonah," Kareem said to him, staring at him strangely, "we have all finished praying for now. Hai Ling was just . . . sharing with the rest of us, how she was having a . . . er . . . difficult time concentrating on her prayer."

Hai Ling launched into a breathless tirade that would have made a Hollywood diva proud, on how boring and useless that whole exercise was. Kareem thumbed his chin and listened patiently, but he continued to cut his eyes back toward Jonah.

Jonah ran his fingers through his hair, telling himself that he was back in the room with the others now. Finally, his heart seemed to slow down and he was able to catch his breath. It wasn't real.

"Anyone else want to share what they experienced?" Kareem eyed Jonah again, but he remained quiet. The faces . . . the eyes . . . and what was with the neon word? All of it haunted his thoughts.

"No one?" Kareem said. "Okay, then let's continue on . . ."

With that, he began with an overview of what they would be discussing in his class. They were, of course, meeting in this smaller room because he was human, and this was a more out-of-the-way place for them to meet without getting caught.

He began talking about the early church, and the things they used to do to develop their ability to listen to God. Not only prayer, but silence and solitude, reading the Scriptures, encouraging one another, and fasting—these were all what Kareem called the spiritual arts.

"There are many of these spiritual practices men and women have used to draw near to Elohim throughout the centuries," he said. "It is a great privilege for us to learn these skills together. Trust me when I say that you have no idea yet what these can do for you, and how they might help you in battle."

Frederick rolled his eyes again when the pastor wasn't looking, but this time Kareem must have sensed it. "You have something to add, Frederick?" he said as he spun toward the boy.

"Well . . ." His sudden movement had momentarily thrown Frederick off, but he quickly composed himself. "I just don't see how all of this is going to help us. I mean, shouldn't we be practicing our archery more, or defense? Or, like, karate or using swords or something?"

Hai Ling was nodding along in agreement, which only stoked the fires for the arrogant boy.

Kareem said nothing for a minute, scratching his goatee, appearing to seriously consider Frederick's comments.

"I hear you, Frederick. There is courage in your voice—perhaps along with a little bit of overconfidence—but courage nonetheless."

This brought even more of a scowl to Frederick's face.

"One way or another," Kareem said to all of the students, "you will each discover that prayer is not only a vital weapon in your arsenal—it is an absolutely necessary part of life itself."

He reached into his pocket and pulled out his phone to check the time.

"It appears as though our class time is over," he said. "You may join Mrs. Aldridge now in the main reading room. Until tomorrow night."

The students got up to leave, all seemingly in a hurry, except for Jonah.

He waited until the others had walked out into the hallway and were reentering the hidden realm, disappearing in front of him like candles snuffed out.

"Reverend Kareem . . . ," he began, but wasn't sure what to say.

The young Pakistani pastor stood up in front of Jonah and looked at him knowingly. "Did you see something . . . interesting?" His eyes glittered as he waited for Jonah to respond.

"Well . . . yes," Jonah said. And in one long sentence, he told his instructor everything he had seen, from the game, to the faces, to the voice. He also told him about missing the shot and the neon word.

Kareem thought for a minute, and then began to move around the room, blowing out the candles as he spoke.

"Entering into a place of prayer with Elohim can be very unpredictable," he said as he moved around to the flames. Jonah watched as the room gradually grew darker, with each light extinguished. "What will you see when you are given up to Him? What will He choose to show you? Every journey is different. Every path is unique. But there is one thing for sure."

Jonah leaned in as Kareem approached the final candle, holding it in front of him.

"If you want to be safe, don't pray."

With that, he blew the final candle out.

TWELVE

THE ANGELIC VORTEX

Jonah joined the others, who had gathered in the center of the reading room and were seated at a few tables. Jeremiah was chatting excitedly with a couple of the kids at his table. Eliza sat quietly beside her roommate Julia, patiently waiting. Her eyes met Jonah's, and she raised her eyebrows at him. By her look, he could tell that he must still look shaken by the vision he had seen during his prayer. Maybe it was something only a sister would notice, but he ran his hand over his face and tried to force his mind back to the present.

"All right, students," Camilla said, standing before them with her usual smile. "Your first night of Angel School is almost complete. Each evening, precisely at fifteen minutes past nine, you will report here, entering the same way you came. I cannot stress the importance of entering the hidden realm before you leave the convent. We don't want to take any unnecessary risks. We have the building and doorways guarded by angels and by the hand of Elohim Himself, of course. But you can never be too careful."

Eliza glanced around at the other kids, adjusted her glasses, and then raised her hand.

"Excuse me, Mrs. Aldridge?" she said. "I was just wondering. Are we going to have grades in Angel School?"

A few of the kids shot her dirty looks. But a couple of others nodded their heads along with her. Jonah just looked at her and rolled his eyes. Leave it to Eliza to want to have grades.

"That's a good question, dear Eliza," said Camilla. "I know how you enjoy making good grades. But we won't have As and Bs like you are used to in school." Eliza raised her eyebrow when Camilla mentioned Bs. Jonah knew she'd never sniffed a B in her life. "No, grades have no use for us here. We expect you to be more motivated by a desire to use your exceptional gifts and to please Elohim in everything."

The angel went on to review what they had learned that night and what they would be doing for their lessons over the next week. She encouraged them to sleep late in the morning, but not to miss their required tutoring classes with the nuns, which would meet at one o'clock. Some of the kids high-fived each other. Jonah had never been asked by a teacher to sleep in before.

"And don't miss a meal either," she said. "A quarterling will be no good in battle if he or she is not rested and well-fed."

She raised her hand and popped herself on the head. "Ah! And I almost forgot . . . before we leave tonight, there is one more thing. From time to time, you will have an opportunity to receive updates from your parents."

Jeremiah fist-pumped the air. A wave of chatter rushed over the room.

She continued, "You will be able to check in with your guardian angels. Even though you cannot talk face-to-face with your parents right now, you can at least find out how they are doing."

She motioned to Samuel now. "Instructor Samuel?"

He nodded his head, stepped forward, and began giving the students instructions. Soon, they were each standing with an angel in different parts of the room, spread out from one another. Brothers and sisters were together, of course, so Jonah, Eliza, and Jeremiah stood in the corner of the room. The warrior angel Taryn stood with them.

"Of course, we know that Henry is a warrior angel now," she said. "But he was among the angels who transported your parents to their secure location, and with Cassandra not having been recovered yet, his assignment involves checking on them frequently. We figure you'd like to know how they're doing."

"I've been thinking about them all day," said Jeremiah. Jonah realized he felt the same, even though he didn't want to admit it out loud. In the middle of everything that had happened that day, his parents had constantly been in the background of his mind.

Taryn nodded. "Okay, then. Ready?" Jonah wasn't exactly sure what he should get ready for, but they each said yes and watched the fire-haired angel raise her hands and close her eyes.

Within seconds, wind began to swirl around them and their hair began to blow wildly, although Jonah noticed that it didn't blow any of the books or papers around the library. It was like a mini-tornado, swirling around the four of them until they couldn't see outside its walls. Strangely, though, it made no noise at all. Jeremiah stood between Jonah and Eliza, holding both of their hands tightly.

Taryn finally opened her eyes. "This is an Angelic Vortex. It is how we communicate with each other around the world." She closed her eyes again, concentrating. Suddenly, in front of them, a large image began to appear on the Vortex. It was fuzzy at first, but grew clear and focused.

"Henry!" said Eliza. The teenage-looking warrior angel faced them, offering them a smile and a wave.

"Hi there, everyone!" said Henry. "All of the Stone kids at once. Wonderful!"

"Henry!" Jonah said. "It's good to see you again."

Henry appeared to be standing on a darkened street or in an alleyway somewhere. It was impossible to know exactly where he was from the image in front of them.

"Hi, Henry!" said Jeremiah. "This is awesome!"

Henry grinned at the boy. "I know, Jeremiah. Pretty cool, huh? Just like being inside a tornado. Well, almost."

Eliza spoke up again. "So how are Mom and Dad doing, Henry? What can you tell us?"

"Yes, well," he began, "they are safe and sound. We made it here to our secure location undercover, and it seems we weren't noticed by any of the Fallen or anyone else they might have working for them. They are hidden away. Quite concerned about the three of you, of course. But they are doing very well."

"Do they miss us?" said Jeremiah. He blinked at the image of the angel in front of him, his face growing serious.

"Yes, Jeremiah," Henry said, his smile fading a little. "Of course they do. They hated leaving you today, and if it had been up to them, they would be with you tonight. But listen, guys, it is better this way right now. It is much easier to keep you all safe."

Henry looked off to the right for a few seconds, as if he were listening to someone else. "Yes, sir," he said. "Right away, Commander."

He turned back toward Taryn and the three Stone kids. "I have to go, friends. But I'm glad we got to talk. I miss seeing your faces."

Jonah found that he missed his friend Henry too. "Hey, Henry," he said, leaning forward a little, clearing his throat. "I . . . we . . . feel the same way."

"I know, dear friend," Henry said quietly, smiling broadly again. "Just remember, you are safe there, guarded by the top battalion of angels, and they are providing high-security protection twenty-four hours a day, seven days a week." He laughed enthusiastically. "You're safer than you were at home, trust me."

Jonah wanted to ask Henry about his vision, to get his thoughts, his take from an angel perspective. But now wasn't the time. He just didn't feel like getting into it with Eliza, or running the risk of scaring Jeremiah, who was brand-new at all of this angel stuff.

"Okay, Henry," Jonah said, willing himself not to worry anymore about what he had seen. Or thought he had seen. "I hope we can see you soon. Tell Mom and Dad we miss them."

Henry nodded and smiled.

"Okay, kids, time to go," said Taryn. She glanced at the angel. "Henry."

He waved good-bye. She dropped her arms, and immediately, the Angelic Vortex was gone. Jonah looked around at the others. Some were still hidden inside their funnels, while others were standing in the reading room, waiting to be dismissed.

Quickly, the students compared stories. It seemed that everyone's parents were safe and doing just fine. They were all worried about their children, and even though most of the kids tried to pretend they didn't miss them back, Jonah knew that wasn't true.

Even Frederick and Hai Ling seemed genuinely moved by their conversations. Only Rupert Clamwater had something negative to say.

"My father demanded to speak directly with me, and he says we aren't safe here, and that the truth is that the angels are not as competent at security as MI5 or the FBI. He says that he can't believe that we are in the middle of New York City and that he is going to file a compl—aaaaah!"

Andre, the quarterling from Russia, had grabbed the back of Rupert's collar, stopping him in midsentence and lifting him off the ground.

"Can you please stop your mouth from moving so much?" the big Russian said, snapping his fingers together with his other hand, mimicking a mouth. "It's hurting my ears!"

Jonah and several of the others cracked up laughing.

"Okay, students. It's time to return to the convent for the night." Camilla ushered them to the doorway, back down the steps, and out of the library, the same way they'd come in.

Jonah yawned as they walked home. The group had grown quiet. He realized for the first time that night how tired he was. All he wanted to do when he got back to his room was get under the covers and melt into the mattress.

THIRTEEN

DAGON'S PLAN

A handful of men and women, dressed in business suits and smart outfits, stood in the conference room, each alone with his or her own thoughts. Some gazed vacantly through the massive set of windows, out across the city. The top floor of the beautiful skyscraper had been rented for them—one of the best views in town—but no one seemed to be enjoying it.

Others paced around the massive mahogany table in the middle. They straightened their ties once, twice, three times. They adjusted their perfect hair. No one spoke. Their usual bickering and blaming was gone. They only waited.

A door swung open at the end of the room, and everyone turned at once.

A few sighs of relief could be heard. An African American man dressed in dingy coveralls pushed a trash can on wheels into the room. His back was bent, and he stared at the floor as he walked in, acting as if he were unaware of the presence of the others.

"I believe you're in the wrong room," one man said with a cold stare, ready to usher this unfortunate man on. Or maybe torment him while they bided their time.

But the janitor simply chuckled. And then they knew.

A collective gasp, and then a woman hit the floor on her knees.

"Master," she said, bowing low.

The others quickly followed her lead, not daring to let their eyes meet the face of the janitor.

"I . . . I didn't . . . ," the one who had tried to expel him a few seconds ago trembled.

A hand landed on his shoulder. "Get up," the janitor said. "All of you, get up."

The janitor plopped down in a tall leather chair at the end of the table and threw his feet up on the dark wood. He smoothed out his coveralls, which had a name tag that said "Dante." He folded his hands behind his short-cropped, wiry hair and then motioned to the empty chairs without a word. The rest quickly found a place to sit.

He ran his hands over his head again, and his hair suddenly became stringy and long, covering half of his face. His eyes turned slowly from dark brown to the color of blood.

"You all look so beautiful today," he said, his eyes falling slowly on each of them. They had to do everything in their power not to shield themselves from his awful gaze. "But I'd rather see you as you really are."

He waved his arm across the room. Instantly they each began to transform. Crusty, gnarled faces emerged, replacing their chiseled features. Crumpled wings sprouted out of their backs.

"There. That's more like it," Abaddon said with a smile. "Your true, ugly, hopeless selves."

He leveled his gaze at them again, turning slowly to look at each one, each of the Fallen who had failed him.

In a strangely calm voice, he spoke. "I gave you a simple task to complete. All I asked was that you destroy the nephilim and their families. How hard could it be?" He chuckled again, allowing the tension to hang in the air. "And you are supposed to be my leaders..."

They were wilting under his terrible stare. His quiet fury was worse than any tongue-lashing he could have given them. He wasn't simply angry—he *was* anger. And it was invisibly pouring out from him, now in its full measure.

Suddenly, as he looked at the fallen angel closest to him, she screamed out in agony and disintegrated into a pile of dust. Slowly, methodically, he turned toward each of them, and each felt the invisible blade slice through them. Soon, they were only piles of black dust on the plush leather chairs.

He rose and watched the tall buildings from the window for a while, his hands behind his back. His eyes veered upward toward the clouds. He glared at something unseen, but said nothing, turning his attention back to the question at hand.

"How will I get rid of the nephilim and their children?"

Yesterday it had been a question of strategy. Of their potential importance to the other side, of how they could be used to stand against Abaddon and his forces. And he had decided he couldn't allow them to live any longer.

Today, though, there was more. Abaddon had been thwarted. Again. His rage did not dissipate in his punishment of the Fallen. It only grew.

"I know a way, Master..."

He didn't turn toward the voice, already knowing who was there.

A young man had entered the room. He wore a black jacket, silk shirt, and jeans with a few holes carefully placed by a pricey designer. His silver-tipped black boots echoed throughout the room as he walked across the wooden floor.

"You know that I should destroy you right now for daring to come into this room, Dagon," Abaddon said. "You're a weasel."

He turned toward the young man and morphed entirely. He was no longer the janitor. His hands and face grew bony and pale. A hood now covered most of his head.

The man lowered his eyes, not daring to look into the Evil One's face. But he had his master's attention, what he had been wanting for some time . . . it was his now, for better or for worse.

Abaddon looked at him with the same glare, but hadn't cast him into oblivion yet with the others. A good sign.

"I can find one of them," Dagon said, eager for his Master to see his ingenuity. "I know how to locate a nephilim for us. I can find out where those . . . *angels* . . . have put one."

He spat the word *angel* with hatred on his tongue.

"And if we find one, I can find out what we need to know," he continued. A personal audience with Abaddon . . . Dagon could barely contain himself.

"The location of the quarterlings," Abaddon said. He paced around again, thinking. "Who will lead us to these children?"

Dagon was ready for this question, and he uttered the name with a proud smirk.

"Clamwater."

Abaddon stared out at the buildings again. Slowly, a smile began to crease his lips. *Roger Clamwater.* He remembered the man's fear and how easily he had collapsed under the power of Marduk last year. He was the first to fall and turn toward the darkness of Abaddon's power. Yes, he was as good a candidate as any. And if they could gain information from him . . .

"He will lead us to the children," said Dagon, his ambition pushing him forward with new energy. "And then they will all come—all of those pathetic creatures will come to the aid of their poor children!"

Abaddon's fist tightened. "Then we will destroy them all."

Dagon nodded. "There is another thing," he said. "But it is small, barely needing my Master's attention. It's just that . . ."

"Get to it, Dagon!" Abaddon snapped.

"Of course, Master. I witnessed a prophet on the streets of New York not long ago."

"So?" the Evil One snarled. "They are of no consequence to us. No one even listens to them these days. Most people think that they're just crazy."

Dagon nodded. "Yes, you are right. It was just that, I happened to see two quarterlings there, listening to her. Jonah and Eliza Stone."

Abaddon spun away from the window and faced him fully now, which caused Dagon to take a couple of steps back. He hadn't expected such a forceful reaction to that family's name.

"There was something between this prophet and the boy," Dagon continued. "In the hidden realm, I could tell there was a . . . connection, between the two."

Abaddon stood in silence for a while, pondering this bit of news, chewing on its significance. "How can you be sure?" he barked.

"I watched them," said Dagon, trying to stand straighter. "I know what I saw, what I heard. There was something there. I could sense it. And I know certain prophets have caused us . . .

problems in the past. At any rate, you should know that we don't have to worry about it going forward."

Abaddon raised his eyebrow. "You killed her?"

"No! Of course not! I wouldn't do that to a prophet without your permission. But I've had her contained," said Dagon, relishing his moment. "She won't in any way be able to interfere with our plans. I am simply trying to cover all the bases."

"And you are telling me this to improve your standing," Abaddon said, bitterness on his tongue as his glare burned into Dagon.

"We will hold her until you are ready to do with her what you wish, my lord."

Dagon bowed his head, knowing better than to say anything else now.

"Yes," Abaddon said, turning his gaze back to the city. He would relish extracting whatever he could from a prophet of Elohim. They were often entrusted with even more useful information than the angels about the movements of His forces. But his thoughts moved back to the boy. If he had a connection with this prophet . . . "This plan to find and rid ourselves of the nephilim," he whispered. "Do it. I'll deal with this prophet later."

Dagon couldn't hide his smile this time as he changed from the young man with the jacket and fancy boots into the demon he truly was. He bowed his head, then snapped his wings once, silently gliding out of the open window of the boardroom.

FOURTEEN

A London Flat

Roger Clamwater walked the fourteen blocks from his office as a stockbroker to his London flat every day, rain or shine. He routinely counted the steps—usually about three hundred every block, totaling somewhere near forty-two hundred—it was something to do on the way home. It helped him ignore the more annoying things—like happy schoolchildren, fresh air, and brightly colored ice-cream parlors.

His mind wandered back to the day before, to the attack, and he shuddered. The spray of bullets from the car driving by had shattered every window of the café where he had been sitting—outside, of course, as was his daily routine in the mornings. He'd been lounging in a chair, reading the *Guardian* and sipping a cup of tea—two lemon slices, no sugar, please—when out of nowhere, shots were fired. Actually, he had heard a scream first. Then glass shattering. A woman behind him dove to the ground, hiding behind a table.

He didn't even have time to react, though. His eyes were

drawn toward the gray compact car driving by. The barrel of a machine gun was sitting on the edge of the passenger door.

Firing.

He forgot to duck. But he remembered certain things in detail. He had dropped his teacup, the porcelain shattering into a million pieces at his feet. There were two hooded figures in the car, one driving and one firing the gun. He felt a breeze blowing through his hair by his ear, just past his side. He would realize later this was from the bullets whizzing by.

The police were there in less than a minute and found Roger still sitting in his chair, staring at the street. The officer shook him to his senses, and he blinked several times, finally seeing the face of the man in front of him.

And then everything began to move at regular speed again, the whole scene before him swirling into focus. He whipped his head around to see people sprawled out around him. There was glass everywhere, tables overturned, a woman with her hand plastered over her mouth, and a bald man sitting in the corner, weeping.

The police had whisked him inside and asked him and a handful of others a thousand questions. What exactly did they see? What kind of car was it? Could they make out a face? What did the gun look like? The truth is, none of them were much help. The whole incident had taken less than ten seconds.

One question topped all of the others, though. It was one they could find no helpful answer for at the moment: why hadn't anyone died?

A few of the officers stood and chuckled to themselves, not wanting to make light of the situation in front of the victims. They made quiet jokes about how bad the aim of the gunman must have been to miss so many people at such short range. Soon some of the others were laughing along with them, marveling at their incredible luck.

Roger had a suspicion that the last thing involved had been luck. He used to believe in luck, but not anymore.

He forced himself to stop counting steps and run his mind back over the incident as slowly as possible. He wasn't sure, but he thought that he might have caught a glimmer of something in the corner of his vision. The gun had been flashing, so he couldn't be sure, but he thought he glimpsed a different kind of flash.

Angel wings?

Of course, once he had been visited later that day by the angels themselves, he knew he must have been right. They had been the ones to shield him and the others from the bullets. They'd been the ones to stop the attack.

They had come to move him, warning him of danger. They told him that not only he but also his son were targets of the Fallen.

It had brought back all the memories from the previous year that he had so carefully locked away: the horrifying places he'd been taken against his will, the creatures he had only had nightmares about before, but now had seen face-to-face. The details of those faces were etched inside of him, somewhere deep. He even remembered their smell, and had found that he couldn't tolerate even a whiff of a scent of garbage now. Taking out the rubbish had become a daily chore.

But there was more. These angels seemed so good. But he didn't trust them. How could he? The only person in his life who had never let him down was his son, Rupert. Everyone else had abandoned him at some point—his mother had died, he'd never met his father, his peers had always made fun of him, and his wife had left after Rupert was born.

Yes, he would send Rupert away, since the angels seemed to have their wings all twisted out of shape about it. He did believe that the threat was real—he had to, since he'd seen it with his own eyes. He would do anything to keep Rupert safe.

But he wouldn't accept their protection for himself. He was determined to continue on as though nothing had happened. His routine, his job, his regular stops at the café—even though they were mundane, they were his. He had only agreed to the angels' protection for his son when it was clear he would get to speak to Rupert, though he had to endure that awful angelic tornado to do it.

There was something else, though. Something he wouldn't tell anyone else.

He remembered what it felt like.

Last year, he had discovered what it felt like to give in to him. The awful, evil, intoxicating feeling of power. He had seen it in Marduk's eyes. He had felt it course through his soul, even for that brief moment.

He hadn't been able to forget the whispers inside his head. Whispers reminding him that Abaddon, the Evil One, could give him all the power he could ever need to protect himself and Rupert forever. With that kind of power, he would never need anyone else again.

Roger continued counting steps, all the way to forty-two hundred. He turned to walk up the steps and into his flat.

It felt smaller with Rupert gone. He sensed the emptiness around him and sighed, dropping his old leather satchel on the dining room table. The place was spotless, just as he liked it. The thought zipped through his mind that he would now be able to keep it much neater without Rupert around. As soon as he thought it, though, he felt a tinge of regret. The loneliness was a fog hanging over every room in the house.

He threw a frozen dinner into the microwave and hit Play on his answering machine. Thirteen messages. He listened to them patiently as he waited for his food. One was from the London Fire Brigade for fund-raising. Delete. The other twelve were from various news agencies looking for interviews about "the alleged terrorist attack" on the café.

He deleted them all and leaned against the kitchen counter. Covering his eyes with his hand, he felt tears begin to flow as he pressed against them. His chest heaved for a few seconds, but he flung the tears away from his face angrily, forcing himself to stop. He never cried, and he wasn't about to start now.

Even by himself.

Roger didn't bother to turn on the light in the den. He plopped down on the creaky sofa and ate his meal in the dark.

The chill that entered the room was barely noticeable at first. And with the steaming plastic tray of meat and noodles on his lap, it took him a little while to figure out what the other smell in his house was.

Maybe he had forgotten to empty the rubbish bin last night. In all of the commotion, he was sure this easily could have happened.

He made a move to get up and check on both the temperature and the trash, but he sat back down again. It was as if a weight were across his chest. He just couldn't bring himself to get off the sofa. He felt so tired. Maybe he just needed to get some extra rest.

He placed the half-empty tray on the floor and lay down flat on the sofa. He felt so tired that he couldn't even reach down to untie his shoes. He was barely able to loosen his tie and undo the top button on his shirt. Folding his arms across his chest, he closed his eyes.

∽

It was easy for Dagon to slip past the six angels keeping watch over the London flat. Easier than he had imagined it would be. He simply had a couple of his associates create a stir in the alleyway across the street—basic diversion tactics.

Elohim's angels really are getting sloppy, he thought. *Of course, maybe I'm just that good.*

He silently watched Roger prepare his food, listen to his messages, and break down crying. *Pathetic,* he thought. *What a weak-willed lowlife.* He saw the dimly lit glow coming from the center of his chest. *If he only knew.* He couldn't help but grin. *He has no idea . . .*

Roger sat down on the sofa. Dagon was beside him as soon as he sank into the cushions. *Time to get to work.* He dug into his shoulders, finding just the right spot. This was the part of his job he relished the most. The other fallen angels could make war with arrows and swords and intimidation. But Dagon knew where the real war was fought—and right now, he was on the front lines.

It took only a few minutes for Roger to fall into a deep sleep. The fallen angel continued his work, whispering into his ear. Roger moved restlessly on the sofa, sweat breaking out on his forehead.

In the nightmare Dagon painted, Roger found himself in a black pit. Dark sludge covered the sides, which made it impossible to climb out on his own. He tried, but he couldn't scale the walls—each time he just slid back down into the dirt. A light appeared above, and he somehow knew instantly what it was, or rather, Who. *That's Elohim*, he thought in his dream. When the hand extended down from the light and into the pit, Roger wavered for a minute.

But slowly, he found himself shoving his hands into his pockets. He couldn't bring himself to take it. He wasn't sure he could trust that hand, or where it would lead him.

The light faded, and for just a moment, a feeling of crashing loss overtook him. Then he saw another hand. It was dark and scaly, but it looked strong. Above it, two eyes pierced through the darkness. He looked into them and found he couldn't look away. There was something in them that was familiar. He'd peered into eyes like this before. Where was it? He struggled to remember.

They drew him in. No words were said, but with every second that passed, Roger heard the promises the eyes spoke. They promised enough power to protect Rupert from anything. They promised to give his son everything he deserved in life. Maybe even enough power to wash all his fears away.

In a moment that caused him to tremble with both ecstasy and horror, he grabbed the hand. Whether it pulled him up and out of the pit, or simply joined him down in it, he was unable to tell.

FIFTEEN

A NEW GIFT

Where am I? What am I doing here?

Those first few seconds of waking up made him feel disoriented. *Was what happened last night just a dream?*

His answer came as he turned his head and saw his tall African roommate sitting cross-legged across the room on his bed, his dusty old Bible on his lap. David's eyes were focused on the page in front of him, so much that he didn't even look up as Jonah moved.

Jonah turned to look at the alarm clock. 11:43. Whoa. He had slept late. But then again, he hadn't dragged himself under the covers until almost three o'clock.

He rolled over and reached underneath his bed. His hand brushed against his own Bible and he pulled it out. Flipping the pages over, he began to read in the Psalms. Over the last year, since the spiritual world had become so real to him, he had found himself searching the Scriptures more and more. At first he was just looking for answers. Seeking out information about the angels, the Fallen, nephilim, and himself.

But he began to find that the more he read, the more he wanted to read.

He found himself in Psalm 20. He glanced back up at David, who now seemed to be praying quietly. Jonah's fingers traced the words, and he let them seep into his heart.

Some trust in chariots, and some in horses;
but we will remember the name of the LORD our God.

The name of the Lord our God. Elohim. Strong One. His dad's favorite name for God. He mulled over those words for a few minutes.

Whatever happens, I trust in You today,
Elohim. I put my trust in You.

Jonah grabbed the first clothes he could find and rushed through a shower so he and David could head down for a bite to eat before school.

The smell of whatever meal was being cooked now wafted down the hallway, and Jonah's stomach growled. About half of the other kids had already arrived in the dining hall when Jonah and David sat down at a table covered with bowls full of heaping helpings of scrambled eggs and hash browns.

"Jonah!" Jeremiah said loudly, hopping down from his seat and running over to give him a hug. Jonah rolled his eyes but hugged his brother back. "I'm already on my second plate! This food is the best!"

"Good, Jeremiah," Jonah said as Julia and Lania, who were sitting nearby, giggled. "It sure does smell good, that's for sure."

"I guess this is breakfast," said David, wide-eyed as he looked at all of the food. "I don't think I've ever eaten breakfast at noon."

"I can't believe you two like that stuff," Jonah said as he took a big swig of orange juice and looked at David's and Eliza's coffee mugs in disgust. Eliza poured a dash of cream and some sugar into her steaming cup, but David left his black. They dug into their plates.

"One day when you grow up a little, you'll love coffee, Jonah," she said, raising her mug to him and smiling. She clinked it against David's and they both took sips.

When everyone had finished breakfast, they made their way into makeshift classrooms the nuns had arranged on the first floor. There the quarterlings were arranged by age—Jonah, David, Frederick, Lania, and Andre; Eliza, Julia, Rupert, Hai Ling, and Ruth; Jeremiah, Bridget, Lania's younger sister, and Carlo, the younger brother of Julia. After several hours of listening to lectures about photosynthesis and quadrangles, and reading *The Pilgrim's Progress* together with only a short break for dinner, Jonah's group emerged a little cross-eyed and more than ready to get back to the library for another session of Angel School.

That evening, at 8:55, the quarterlings made the quiet trek from the convent to the New York Public Library in the hidden realm. The angels stood, vigilant as ever, on the tops of the buildings around them.

"Good evening, students!" Camilla said as they walked into the main reading room. "I hope you are all ready for an educational evening together." The students nodded their heads obediently, bowing their heads as she opened their session with prayer.

"Now," she said, looking at each of them carefully. "Listen, my friends. Who can tell me Ephesians 6:12?"

Before anyone else could even think, Eliza's hand shot up. "For our struggle is not against flesh and blood, but against the rulers, against the authorities, against the powers of this dark world and against the spiritual forces of evil in the heavenly realms."

Camilla smiled. "Excellent, dear Eliza."

Jonah sighed, kicking himself for not answering faster. If there was any passage he knew, it was that one, since it had been so important to him and Eliza last year.

"Now," Camilla continued, clapping, "something new. Taryn, will you come forward, please?"

Taryn obediently stepped in front of the group and into the middle of the floor.

"That same place in the Scriptures speaks of other gifts," the warrior angel said. "Some of which have been manifested here, and some that are yet to be."

The students whispered to one another. Would they be learning to use another gift? And whom did it belong to?

Taryn placed her hands on her head, concentrating with her eyes closed. Within seconds, her helmet appeared. Jonah and Eliza had seen it before, but the others hadn't, and either way, it was impressive. Made out of some kind of dark metal, there were etchings all over it that looked like words in a foreign tongue. Jonah suspected it was the angelic language.

"Wow!"

"Awesome!"

The quarterlings couldn't contain themselves or take their eyes off it.

"The helmet of salvation," announced Taryn. "As those with angelic blood, there are some of you who will have this gift."

She looked back at Camilla, who was thumbing through her little leather book.

"Let's see ... yes ... there it is." She looked up briefly, meeting eyes with all of the students, and began to call names. "Bridget."

Bridget stepped forward, smiling.

"Carlo. Rupert."

The boys looked at each other curiously as they came forward. Rupert still managed to wear a scowl, though.

"And ... Eliza."

Jonah spun his head toward his sister, who couldn't contain the grin on her face. She took her place beside the other three.

"First things first," Taryn said. "You need to learn to make it appear. Then we can discuss how it is used most effectively in battle. But let me warn you, it's not as easy as it looks."

She instructed them to place their fingertips lightly on both sides of their head and concentrate on Elohim. "Ask Him for the protection of your mind," she said. "And then just let the helmet come."

She said it as if it were as easy as brushing your teeth, or breathing. But as the kids did what she asked, Jonah could tell it was going to take some practice.

An image of a helmet flickered around Bridget's and Carlo's heads. It was there, and then it wasn't, then it reappeared. The more Carlo scrunched his face, concentrating, the more his helmet flickered.

Rupert tried and tried. His helmet flickered once, but he became so frustrated so quickly that he threw his hands down in disgust, muttering to himself.

It didn't surprise Jonah at all that Eliza had the best result on her first try. The helmet around her head was faint, but visible, and didn't flicker at all.

"Excellent, Eliza!" exclaimed Taryn. "Wonderful for a first attempt."

Jonah watched her as she stood in front of everyone, her cheeks blushing. He had to admit that he was impressed by his little sister.

"All right," said Camilla, clapping her hands again. "Eliza, Bridget, Carlo, and Rupert, you'll practice the helmet of salvation individually later with your other combat gifts within your groups. Now everyone head to your classes, quarterlings."

In Angelic Combat, Jonah's group worked on arrows again. Marcus and Taryn were sticklers for the details and spent a lot of time teaching them how to stand, where to place their hands on the bow, the most effective way to aim, and even how to breathe when firing. All of it was important, Taryn said, for their accuracy. But the others seemed to learn faster than he did. Even Hai Ling hit close to the bull's-eye tonight, and she found herself squealing with delight for a few seconds, before she remembered to act sullen and bored again.

Frederick was the best, of course. He hit the bull's-eye dead-on twice, earning applause from Taryn, and even a smile from the stone-faced Marcus. Jonah forced himself to congratulate him, even though he had to do it through clenched teeth.

Inside, though, he stewed. He had hit the target every time, which Taryn had told him was something to build on. But he never came close to the red center.

In Scriptural Studies with Samuel, they spent a lot of time on the book of Genesis, and David continued to stand out as someone with a great knowledge of the Scriptures. Jonah couldn't help but be impressed as his roommate answered every question Samuel threw at him about the first book of the Bible. Samuel spent quite a bit of time in Genesis 6.

"Verse 4: 'The Nephilim were on the earth in those days—and also afterward—when the sons of God went to the daughters of humans and had children by them. They were the heroes of old, men of renown.'"

Jonah raised his hand. "Samuel, were you there during those times? You know, before the Flood? What was it like?"

Samuel looked down at his podium for a minute, as if composing himself. His face grew dour, and he looked at the wall behind his students as he spoke. "I was around, yes, Jonah. I saw many awful, horrifying things. All men carry the potential for great darkness, and nephilim even more so, because of their great power. But I saw many heroic acts as well, which people often forget when speaking of the nephilim. All power can be used for good or evil. And therefore," he said, drawing his gaze down to the students again, "you have been given an important choice, my quarterling friends. For you also have great power, and must decide how you will use it."

Jonah felt the weight of Samuel's words on his shoulders. Even though he was only fourteen, he had seen the results of people using power for good, as well as evil. He wondered if, in the heat of the moment, he would be able to make the right choices with the power he had. And what about his friends?

He let his eyes drift slowly over the others in the room. David, Lania, Hai Ling. Then to Frederick, chewing on a fingernail, with an unreadable expression on his face.

And suddenly the weight on Jonah's shoulders felt even heavier.

SIXTEEN

A VIVID DREAM

Help me..."

Jonah heard the words, spoken almost in a moan, before he saw anything. A strong wind was blowing, and the voice was just above it, just a little louder, riding along from wherever it came from into Jonah's ear. It sounded as if it was the voice of someone in pain, someone almost too weak to call out.

Jonah listened to the voice cry for help in the darkness, and somehow he recognized that there was something peculiar about it.

He had heard this voice before. But as hard as he tried, he couldn't place it. Yet it connected with something deep inside him. The voice struck a chord within him, both enchanting and disturbing.

"Help me..."

It came again, with urgency, and it tore into Jonah's heart, bringing questions crashing through his mind. *Where is this voice coming from? Why do I recognize it? Who is calling out for help?*

Then his eyes were suddenly opened and he was moving in the air, flying through the space between cloud and skyscraper, hovering over an enormous city. He barely avoided a giant spire sticking up off the roof of a building. He couldn't control where he was going, and whether he was flying himself or someone else was pulling him along, he couldn't tell. All he could see were the tops of buildings flashing by.

He heard the cry again and felt his heart speed at the sound of the voice. It was growing louder. Maybe he was getting closer. His eyes moved as quickly as they could as he flew, searching. It seemed like he was moving south, but he wasn't totally sure. Up ahead, beyond the buildings, he thought he caught a silver flash of water.

"Help . . ."

The strain in the voice wrecked Jonah. It wasn't just feeling sorry for someone who was in trouble. In that instant, he felt a desire, almost a calling, to do whatever he could to help. Not that he simply *wanted* to or felt that he *should*. It was as if he was supposed to help.

He *had* to help.

And then, even though he wanted to continue searching until he found the source of the voice, he began to float upward, away from the city. He reached down desperately, but nothing he could do controlled his flight. White wisps of cloud began to pass in front of him, blocking his view of the ever-diminishing buildings below. Soon all he could see was the white cotton of a cloud bank all around him.

Jonah jerked as his eyes popped open. It took him at least a minute to realize where he was. Back in his bed.

He pushed his covers off violently, which were damp with his sweat. He propped himself up on his elbows and sat very still.

He listened, straining to hear the words from his dream. But all he heard was the steady breathing of his roommate and the distant noise of cars passing by a few blocks away.

He couldn't shake the feeling he had. That this wasn't just a dream. Someone was in trouble. *"Help me."* The words coursed through his mind. He placed his hand over his heart and felt it racing still.

Finally, Jonah rolled over on his side toward the wall and tried to go back to sleep. How could he help someone when he didn't know where they were—other than New York City some-where—and didn't know who the voice belonged to? He couldn't even leave the convent. And no one would believe that it was anything more than a silly dream anyway.

He tried to close his eyes again, but as soon as he did, another thought occurred to him, and they popped open again. In his grogginess from the dream, he hadn't connected the dots until now.

The voice—it was the same one that he'd heard in his vision the night before.

SEVENTEEN

CHALLENGE TO A DUEL

W hat's the deal with you?" said Eliza that morning at breakfast, immediately picking up on his different demeanor.
"You look a little bit . . . disoriented."

Jeremiah looked up from his plate of eggs, bacon, and biscuits
and cocked his head to the side as he studied Jonah. He shoved
in another mouthful of eggs as he continued to watch his older
brother carefully.

Jonah shrugged, running his hands through his uncombed
hair as he fell into the chair. "Just a weird dream last night."

Eliza put her fork down and turned toward him. "Just a
dream . . . or a *vision*?"

Jonah sighed, accepting the fact that she wasn't going to let
him off the hook until he talked to her.

He relayed the dream with as many details as he could
remember.

"Sounds like this person, whoever it is, is in the city somewhere," she said, mulling everything over. "Which way were you heading? North? South? Could you make out any street signs?"

He sighed, knowing it would be impossible for her to talk about anything else now. "Maybe. It kind of felt like I was going south. I remember seeing a huge spire on the roof of a building, and then some water. But there was something in the first one too."

"*What?*" Eliza grabbed his arm. "There was more than one vision? Okay, we're not going anywhere until you fill me in."

Jonah could see that there was no avoiding telling Eliza the truth. And he didn't really feel like finding out what would happen if he made her late for their daily tutoring session, so he took a deep breath and told her everything about the basketball game vision he could remember. Including the pink neon word he saw on the scoreboard. She was just as baffled as he was.

"Jonah," Eliza said, looking at him intensely, "do you think that the voices were the same?"

"They sounded exactly the same. But listen, Eliza. That doesn't mean much. Maybe I was just dreaming about the vision I had— which probably doesn't mean anything anyway—and the voice showed up there too." He heard himself trying to explain it away, but he wasn't even sure that he bought his own explanation. He knew that she wouldn't.

"So what are you going to do about it?"

"I missed the shot . . . ," he said, almost to himself. Why had he missed the game-winning shot and let everyone down? What did that mean?

Jonah needed time to think, to be alone, to work through things. Picking up his bowl without a word, he set it over with the other dirty dishes in the corner and walked out of the dining hall.

He found himself wandering along the first-floor halls of the convent. They were empty and quiet, and walking slowly through them gave him some time to try to sort through everything. He tumbled the visions around in his mind, like his mom's washing machine did with his dirty gym clothes, spinning and churning them every which way.

Jonah heard the distant voices of kids playing some type of game, and he knew they were in the small, secluded courtyard of the convent, probably playing dodgeball. It was the only place outside that Camilla would allow the quarterlings to go. He walked the other way, running his hand along the hallway walls.

He came to the hall along the back of the convent, and his eyes were immediately drawn to the four windows along the wall. They were simple, square windows, but instead of clear glass, each was fitted with a detailed stained glass image. Jonah was immediately reminded of their church at home, All Souls United Methodist, and the stained glass windows in the sanctuary. These were smaller and not as detailed, but brought a colorful, warm light into the hallway. There were titles underneath each— Peter, James, John, and Jesus. He was drawn most strongly to the picture of Jesus. It wasn't an image he'd seen before, like Jesus as a shepherd or on the cross. It was Jesus, standing in front of the empty tomb, holding a set of keys in his hand, his other arm raised, his face fierce and victorious.

Jonah stood in front of it for a while, then placed his hand on the latch at the bottom of the window. To his surprise, the mere touch of his hand pushed the window slightly open. The latch was broken. He pushed it open a bit more and found himself looking out into the alleyway behind the convent.

I *should mention this to one of the nuns so they can get it fixed,* he thought as he pulled the window shut again and hurried downstairs, realizing it was time to catch up with the others.

The uncomfortable feeling he had seemed to grow over the course of the afternoon. If anything, the time passing only made him feel more confused, and more urgent, about the voice. If someone really was in trouble, shouldn't he try to do something about it? What if he was the only one who could hear it? Was he going to be too late? Was the clock running down, just like his vision?

The only time he was able to get his mind off the voice was during Angelic Combat class that evening. Marcus and Taryn spent their usual time on shooting arrows. They also had begun to work with Jonah's group on the sandals of speed, since they all shared that gift too. They ran around a makeshift track set up along the walls of the large room. To even the angels' surprise, Hai Ling was the fastest of the bunch.

"It's all right, Jonah," said Taryn, noticing Jonah's discouragement. "No one can be the best at everything. Every quarterling has a unique set of gifts. Kind of like a fingerprint."

"I don't seem to be gifted at anything," Jonah replied. He held his hands up in frustration. "Hai Ling is faster. And I thought I was a pretty good archer, but I can't hit anything I aim at, especially compared to Frederick."

"Jonah," said Taryn in a soft voice. She moved closer to him so that only he could hear her. "You have special qualities that are different from anyone else here. You may not know this, but you were the first among the quarterlings whom Elohim allowed to discover your powers. Think about that for a minute."

Jonah just stared at his feet, but he did allow himself to think about what she was saying. Marcus walked past him, focused in his conversation with Lania, and bumped Jonah on the shoulder.

"Watch where you're going!" Jonah lashed out angrily, pushing the big angel right back.

Marcus glared at Jonah and suddenly pulled his sword from the side of his hip—a blazing, golden sword that appeared longer than Jonah was tall. Jonah was still in shock when Marcus charged at him. At the same time, the angel yelled what Jonah could only imagine was a warrior's battle cry. It caused all of the students, now gathered on the edges of the space, to shudder and step back.

Instinct took over. Jonah grabbed at his side like Marcus had, making a pulling motion as if he were drawing a sword. Some of the students gasped as a real, gleaming sword appeared in his right hand.

Jonah's angelblade.

The sword Marcus wielded was golden, with flames licking across its surface, but Jonah's was more silver in color. Shorter, it was light and sleek in his hands, and instead of flames, it emitted a silvery glow. It was the perfect size and weight for its owner.

Marcus, with the help of a flap of his majestic wings, was right in front of Jonah now. With a wild look in his eyes, he brought his blade crashing down. Jonah fell back onto the stone floor, and just in time, he raised his blade, blocking the angel's blow.

A brilliant white flash filled up the room as the swords met. Sparks exploded all around Marcus and Jonah. He anticipated a burning sensation as they fell onto his arms, but instead, they were cool when they touched his skin and melted away immediately.

Quickly, from his position on the ground, Jonah raised his foot and shoved it into the big angel's stomach. Summoning all the angel strength he could muster, he pushed. He caught Marcus off balance, flinging him over his head so that he stumbled for a few feet and fell to one knee.

Jonah sprang up off the ground and turned toward Marcus.

Crouching with the sword in front of him, everyone in the room but the massive angel vanished from his view. There was a gleam in Jonah's eye now.

Marcus charged Jonah again, but Jonah was ready this time. Marcus swung his blade again and again, but the quarterling met each blow with one of his own. They moved around the room in a circle, trading blows, back and forth, faster and faster. The look of determination grew on Marcus's face as he continued on. But Jonah was focused now as well and ferocious in his attempts to block the attacks.

Incredibly, Jonah began to actually push Marcus back with sword blows of his own, accompanied by an eruption of cheers. The swords crashing together created an indoor electrical storm, with almost blinding light. Jonah continued to advance, raining down blows one after the next. He sensed the retreat of the warrior angel.

Now was his chance.

He willed his feet to move. Instantly, his basketball shoes disappeared, replaced by ancient-looking sandals. Speeding around the large, but slower, angel, he was behind Marcus in a blur. Jonah swung his leg out, meeting the angel's calf and sweeping it underneath him. Marcus crashed to the ground, thudding into the marble floor with the weight of a bulldozer.

He turned over as quickly as he could, but Jonah was faster. He was on top of the angel's chest, his sword pointed at his neck.

"I guess all of the practice has been paying off," Jonah said with a triumphant grin. He hopped off the angel and extended his hand.

A combination of surprise, anger, and embarrassment moved quickly across Marcus's face. He glanced around at the students, though, and reluctantly accepted Jonah's hand up.

"A bit of beginner's luck," said Marcus gruffly. But he held Jonah's hand for an extra few seconds, shaking it. "But nice job, Stone."

Taryn beamed as she moved beside Marcus. "Thank you, Marcus."

Jonah looked confused. "You're thanking him? For attacking me?"

But she only winked at him and walked away.

The students cheered again and then crowded around Jonah, all except Frederick, who stood off to the side, unable to hide his jealousy. Jonah smiled for the first time that day, overwhelmed by his friends offering their congratulations. They peppered him with a thousand questions—"How did you learn how to fight like that?" "How does a quarterling beat an angel in battle?" And most of all, "Where did you get that angelblade?"

It was impossible for Jonah to answer all of the questions, although he tried. When Andre asked how he might earn his own angelblade, it was Taryn who answered.

"Angelblades were simply not given to those who are not fully angel," she said. "Until Jonah Stone came along, of course."

"This is a key principle for all who follow Elohim," Camilla chimed in. "He can do whatever He wants to do, whenever He wants to do it."

She had effectively turned the conversation back to Elohim, and Jonah was grateful. As much as he enjoyed redeeming himself in front of his classmates, he remembered how uncomfortable he felt during his first day at the convent, when he had had the spotlight all to himself. The others backed off him but continued to talk about what they had just witnessed.

"Okay, students," Samuel said, stepping in and looking more

than a little perturbed that class time had been taken away. "Time to get back to our studies. Hurry along now."

The students in Kareem's class reappeared in front of him.

He ushered them back in. "I guess I missed something. Where have all of you been?"

EIGHTEEN

VANISHING ANGELS

Jonah knew he should get some sleep after his long day of classes, but he couldn't calm down enough. Even with his success in the duel against Marcus, he could only think about his vision. How was he supposed to know if it was real? If he needed to do something? When he prayed, it just made him feel restless, like he needed to get up and move. He felt lost.

Not wanting to keep David awake with his tossing and turning, Jonah crept out of their room and over to the window at the end of the hallway. From four stories up, he had a pretty good view of the darkened street below. There were two streetlights visible, but they were barely emanating a glow at all. His eyes grew accustomed to the light, and he began to make out shapes and forms.

His eyes wandered upward, to the tops of the dark buildings. The sky behind them was covered in clouds, blue and gray, reflecting the light from the city. It created its own mysterious, dim glow. Jonah prayed and slipped into the hidden realm so he could make out the angels, like marble statues, standing guard over the convent below. He wondered if they ever moved or changed shifts. He knew angels didn't need sleep like humans did. *They must get so bored, though*, he thought.

He was about to turn away when something caught his eye on the building above. Movement. He blinked, squinting to try to see what was happening. The angel who had been on the end of the building just a few seconds ago was gone.

He stared hard at the empty space. Maybe he had been mistaken. Or perhaps the warrior angel had decided to take a break or check something out that he had seen on the street.

Jonah was still trying to figure out what had happened when he saw a faint, fiery glow on top of the building. The next angel in line suddenly disappeared. It wasn't just that he fell down or was even dragged down. He simply disintegrated.

Before he had time to react, ten more angels along the rooftop met the same fate. Each time there was a flash of red, and then they were gone. He thought he saw white dust blowing off the building and down toward the street.

Behind the angels, other figures emerged. They did not strike the imposing silhouette the angels had. Instead, they were shadows with hunched backs, barely visible against the dark sky. The only light came from the gleam in their yellow eyes.

Jonah felt something inside him grow cold. His throat dried up, and he tried to swallow. He wanted to move, but his legs felt heavy. He continued to watch.

The creatures jumped off the roof, spreading their crumpled, black wings wide, soaring down to the street. They came into view under the street lamp on the ground. Their skin looked charred and blackened, as if they'd been dipped in boiling lava and then yanked out.

Jonah looked frantically up into the sky. Where were the other angels? He knew that there was a whole host of them posted along the top of the convent building too. Where were they? Had they also been attacked?

A wisp of white dust falling right in front of the window answered that question.

Turning down the hallway, he prayed himself back into the physical realm and began to run, banging on every door he came to.

"Get up!" he yelled as loudly as he could. "Everybody, get up! We're under attack!"

Jonah continued banging on the doors, up and down the hallway. They began to open, sleepy boys in their pajamas sticking their heads out.

"Jonah Stone's gone mad," a groggy Rupert Clamwater said. "And there I was, having the nicest dream about tea and Turkish delight . . ."

Another door opened and Frederick stood, arms folded and grumpy. "What are you doing, Stone? We're trying to get some sleep here!"

But Jonah would have none of it. "Get your clothes on and get dressed, all of you, as fast as you can!" he called out to the boys, who were all standing in the hallway now. "We're surrounded by fallen angels, and they're closing in." They still stood, staring, unsure of whether they should believe him. Exasperated, Jonah yelled at them again. "If you don't believe me, go to the window and look for yourselves!"

They tripped over each other to get to the windowsill. Frederick was the first one there, and the first to turn around. No more disdain on his face. It was replaced with both determination and fear.

"You heard what he said, guys!" he commanded the others. "Get dressed and get downstairs!"

They rushed back to their rooms as one. Jeremiah was among them, dressed in his light-blue pajamas with his hair sticking up in every direction. Jonah read the worry in his eyes. He tried to manage a smile for his younger brother.

"It's going to be okay, Jeremiah," he said, knowing how half-hearted he sounded. "Just . . . go ahead and get dressed. We have to go downstairs, okay?"

Jeremiah bit his lip and nodded.

When Jeremiah was ready, Jonah slammed the door of the stairwell open and bounded down the steps three at a time, grateful for the longer legs he'd grown over the last year, thanks to his angelic heritage. After bursting into the third-floor hall, he began banging on the girls' doors too.

Girls started coming out of their rooms, confusion on their faces. Eliza emerged from her room quickly, rubbing the sleep out of her eyes.

"You're up fast," Jonah said, beating on the door across the hall. "Good. Get dressed."

She stared at him as he moved past her, and suddenly she knew. "Fallen angels. They're here."

"You guessed it," he said, banging on another door. "They are everywhere outside. Do me a favor—wake up everybody and get them downstairs!"

"But how did they get past the angels?" she asked, putting her glasses on. "How do they know where we are?"

Jonah had already moved down the hallway. "No time to talk about that now, E. Just get these girls up!"

Jonah heard her switch into command mode and begin

barking orders to the other girls. He knew she would have them downstairs soon. He had no idea what they would do when they got there, but they would be together.

When they reached the first floor, Jonah hurried past the dining hall and toward the meeting room. Four nuns rushed in, entering the prayer room just as he passed it. He glanced over and saw them kneel on the floor together, join hands, and begin to pray.

As he turned the corner, Camilla Aldridge strode down the hallway toward him, followed by Samuel, Marcus, and Taryn. Just behind them was Reverend Kareem, in gym shorts and a T-shirt, shaking the grogginess out of his head.

Camilla saw Jonah and paused. "Did you summon the others?"

"Yes," Jonah said. "They're coming. Camilla, I saw the Fallen overtake the angels on the building. They're all over the pl—"

"Yes, dear, we know," she said bluntly. She turned to Marcus and Taryn. "Guard the entrances, both of you. We will get the students organized and send them to reinforce you."

The two warrior angels nodded, rushing by Jonah. Taryn stood at the door that opened up into the street. She had pulled an arrow from her quiver, bracing herself for whatever was about to come through the door. Marcus hurried down the hallway, half running and half flying to secure the back entrance.

The students were filtering down, rushing into the hallway. They began to move even faster when they saw Marcus flying by them and Taryn positioned at the front door. They glanced at each other as they ran, and the look on their faces was clear.

We really are in danger.

Camilla ushered all of the students into the meeting room, along with Samuel and Kareem.

"There has been a breach in our security," she said, not trying to hide the gravity in her tone. "Our angelic forces have somehow been defeated. It is unclear at this point how, and it is not important at the moment. What is important is that we, together, are prepared to do battle."

Jonah studied the faces of the students, many of whom had become his friends over the past couple of days. None of them had faced even one fallen angel before, let alone a whole company of them. No one could hide that they were scared.

"It will do you no good to worry," said Camilla. "It is times like this when it will do you well to remember that Elohim is always with you. We will trust His strength to carry us through."

Samuel and Kareem murmured together, nodding in agreement. Camilla extended her hand toward the young pastor.

"We angels have agreed to become visible to Kareem, as well as to the nuns in the convent. They will be critical in defending this place." Kareem nodded, stepping forward as Camilla turned toward him and spoke. "Will you select four of your best students to join you and the others in the prayer room?"

"The *prayer room*?" Frederick blurted out. "Seriously? We have fallen angels all over the place outside, breaking right through the angelic barrier that you all said was so safe, and you are worried about us getting our prayer time in?"

"That is quite enough, Frederick!" she said, speaking so fiercely that her face almost began to emit a white-hot glow. He shut his mouth, taken aback by her forcefulness. She caught her breath and took a second to gather her emotions, now speaking in a more measured tone. "You would do well not to speak ill of what you do not fully understand. There is a reason we teach the spiritual arts. You will find that out tonight."

Kareem searched the faces of the students in front of him. "David. Bridget. Carlo. Julia. Come with me."

The four students followed Kareem out of the room.

"We will divide the rest of you up. Some we will send with Marcus, others with Taryn. Others will patrol the hallways with me."

Rupert slowly raised his hand. Everyone in the room could see it shaking as he held it in the air.

"Yes, Rupert?" said Camilla, glancing back toward the doorway. "Make it quick, please."

He looked around at the others, then back at the angel. "Are they really after us? And if they can get through the whole Second Battalion of the Angelic Forces of the West, what makes you think that we can fare any better?"

Camilla looked on him with as much compassion as she could muster in the moment.

"Yes, they are after you, all of you," she said. "And they won't rest until each of you is dead. We have given you all of the protection we possibly can, but we always knew there would be a day when the fight would come directly to you. What we did not expect is that this day would come so soon."

Jonah and the rest of the students already knew this, but hearing her say it carried a new weight.

"Trust, my friends," she said. "Have faith. This is what you were made for, after all."

With that, she began to assign the students to different groups.

She looked at Jonah, Eliza, Jeremiah, and Rupert. "You four are with me. We will patrol the halls. Just because the doorways are secure doesn't mean that we won't find them trying to enter through a window or an air duct. They are wily, desperate creatures."

Camilla whipped around, her blue robe sweeping across the floor, and they followed, trying to keep up with her. Which was hard, considering that she was almost airborne as she strode down the hall.

"Eliza, Rupert—I want you two to patrol the first floor. Check rooms and windows. Locate all of the air vents and monitor them carefully. Do your best." She turned to Jonah and Jeremiah. "You two, on the second floor. Same orders. I will cover the third and fourth floors, and rooftop, if necessary."

Jonah's mind was moving so fast he could barely process it all. That seemed like a dangerous assignment, even for an angel of Camilla's standing. "Don't you think that's a lot for just one angel, Mrs. Aldridge?"

But she was already almost to the stairwell. She didn't take the time to turn around, only waved a hand in the air, dismissing his comment with a flick of her wrist.

"Listen, Jeremiah," he said as they entered the darkened second-floor hallway. "You have to promise me to be careful, and not to do anything stupid. You don't have any defensive powers yet, so stay behind me and let me handle the fighting, okay?"

Jeremiah was already looking down the hallway in each direction, trying to spot a fallen angel. He didn't respond.

Jonah grabbed him by the shoulder, with more force than he intended. "Did you hear me?"

Jeremiah snapped his head back toward Jonah. "All right, let go! I promise, I won't do anything dumb."

"Okay, let's pray," Jonah said. "We can't see the Fallen unless we are in the hidden realm."

They both prayed quietly and slipped into the hidden realm. Jonah drew an arrow and strung it on the bow that had appeared in his hand.

They walked down the hallway slowly, back to back. There was a window on each end of the hallway, and they both kept their eyes on those. But as they walked along, Jonah pushed open each door they came to and did a quick search of the nuns' rooms.

Jonah felt a few drops of nervous sweat roll down his forehead. But he tried to ignore them, and kept his arrow aimed and ready.

It wasn't long until they had covered almost all the hallway. Every room had been searched except for the last two, and so far, there was no sign of a fallen angel.

"I hope Eliza and Rupert are doing okay," whispered Jeremiah.

"Yeah," Jonah said, turning to look at his brother. "I just hope Rupert isn't curled up in a corner somewhere, covering his eyes."

Jeremiah covered his mouth to keep from laughing out loud, and Jonah smiled.

They kicked another door open, Jonah searching the room as quickly as he could while Jeremiah kept watch. The room was sparse and neat, except for the bedsheets that had been thrown onto the floor in haste. These rooms belonged to nuns, and not messy kids, after all. A quick peek at the window and under both beds told Jonah that this room was safe.

When he emerged from the room, Jonah saw Jeremiah standing as still as if he were frozen to the ground. His face was white, and his lips were pressed together firmly. He held a finger up to Jonah and pointed to his ear.

Listen.

Jonah stood quietly beside his brother. In the room across the hallway, the last one left to search, they heard the faintest sound. A creak, and then silence. Another creak. It stopped again.

Footsteps.

Jonah swallowed hard, pulling his arrow back a little farther. Breathing in deeply, he raised his foot off the ground and kicked in the door.

Two creatures stood in front of him, their crusty bodies hunched over. Their yellow eyes grew large with surprise. Their mouths gaped open, showing their sharp teeth, and they howled as they reached for their arrows.

But before they could retrieve their weapons, Jonah let his arrow fly.

Thud!

He strung another one quickly and shot the other creature in the chest.

The fallen angels screeched in agony, so that the boys threw their hands over their ears. The creatures writhed on the floor for a couple of seconds before they turned into black dust and seeped down into the cracks of the wooden floor.

Jeremiah stepped around the dust and walked over to the window. He slammed it shut, snapping the lock in place.

"Nice shot, Jonah!" Jeremiah said, holding out his hand for a high five. Jonah slapped Jeremiah's hand hard, breathing in heavily.

He stepped back into the hallway just in time for a flaming arrow to whiz under his nose, missing him by mere centimeters. As he snapped his head back, another arrow sailed by, just as close, nearly hitting his shoulder before slamming into the door-jamb and disintegrating.

"Jeremiah!" Jonah yelled. "Get back in!"

He pushed his brother back into the room and slammed the door without thinking. But now he was left alone in the dark hall.

Ducking his head low, he ran as fast as he could in the opposite direction of the arrows. Another one zoomed over his head, barely missing him.

He had no plan, and he knew there wasn't a stairwell on this end of the hallway to use as an escape. He pushed open another door and quickly entered the room, shutting the door behind him.

Think, Jonah! He knew they would be coming as fast as they could. And what if they caught Jeremiah in the other room? If they were going to survive, he had better do something and do it now. But the only thing he could think about was his defenseless brother in a room all by himself.

He braced himself and burst back through the door, ready to fire. But no more than five feet away stood a huge fallen angel, leveling his own arrow squarely at Jonah's chest.

Jonah met the glowing yellow eyes with his own. They suddenly narrowed, and he knew that this creature didn't care whether he got shot or not.

"Jonah?"

The Fallen heard the voice from down the hall and took his eyes off Jonah for a split second. It was all the time Jonah needed.

His arrow pierced the fallen one through the neck. He fell to the ground, turned to black ash, and disappeared.

"Well, I can't hit a bull's-eye very well, but I can hit these guys," he muttered to himself.

Jeremiah had peeked into the hallway to check on his brother and now came running toward him.

"Thanks, Jeremiah," Jonah said, smiling.

"I was worried about you out here," he said. "What just happened?"

"You gave me just enough time to get rid of a nasty bad guy."

Jonah reached out his hand and pulled his brother toward him, hugging his head in the crook of his arm.

NINETEEN

THE PRAYER BARRIER

They continued to patrol the hallway, walking back and forth slowly, checking and rechecking the rooms, shutting all of the windows, and placing furniture over the vents, thinking this might at least slow the Fallen down if they tried that route. Jonah glanced out the window every few minutes. Each time he could see more fallen angels swarming around on the ground.

There was no sign of friendly angels anywhere outside. Jonah wondered where they were. Why hadn't reinforcements been sent? What had happened to the defenses that were supposed to be so strong that nothing could penetrate them? How did the Fallen even know where they were?

Was it possible that Abaddon or one of his agents had gotten to one of the nuns in the convent? Or one of the nephilim who knew their location?

"Boys," Camilla called from the end of the hallway. "Come with me. Now."

Jonah relayed their encounters with the Fallen.

"Nice work, gentlemen," said their commanding angel. "You are both to be commended for your bravery. I had quite a scuffle upstairs myself." She brushed some dust off her sleeve. "But it's taken care of, at least for the moment."

"Where are we going?" Jonah asked as they stood with her in the darkness. "I thought you wanted us to guard the second floor."

She motioned to them to come back down the stairs with her. "It appears as though we have withstood the first series of attacks. Your friends and sister also fought off the Fallen with much courage. They cannot get through, thanks to the efforts of the prayer group. I have no doubt that there will be another attack. But for now, we need to go see the others."

Jonah and Jeremiah obediently followed her down the steps and into the small prayer room. A table that used to be in the center of the room had been moved aside, and the nuns, Kareem, and the four students he had selected knelt in a circle. They were murmuring softly with their eyes closed, each of them pleading with Elohim in his or her own way for His protection of the convent.

Jonah was impressed with how intense their prayers were, but what was really cool was what it looked like as he viewed it in the hidden realm. White, glowing tendrils of light rose upward from each member of the circle. Some had three or four ropes of this light extending from their chests; a few had more. Kareem and Sister Patricia must have had dozens between them.

The fingers of light stretched just above their heads and then did something that caused Jonah to look closely. They touched one another, intertwining to form a beautiful, brilliant circle above their heads and extending through the ceiling above. It seemed that once the individual tendrils connected together, they glowed much brighter than when they were alone. Their combined efforts produced something powerful and captivating.

Eliza and the others who had been patrolling had joined them too, standing alongside Jonah and Jeremiah. They looked just as awestruck as Jonah felt.

"The prayer of a righteous person is powerful and effective," Camilla said, smiling. Jonah had heard that passage of the Bible before.

"I never thought of it like this," he admitted.

Camilla nodded. "The united prayer of believers is a powerful force in the hidden realm. It is much more powerful than humans realize. One person can cause tremendous change in the course of certain events. And a group of people united together for a common cause . . ." She spoke in awe of its power. It struck Jonah that she spoke of prayer the way he often found himself speaking of angelic powers. An angel, amazed by something a human could do?

"Their prayers for protection are forming a barrier around this convent. We withstood the first run from the Fallen not only because of your fighting abilities but also because of their prayers. A few of the fallen ones got through, but we have taken care of those."

Jonah looked at the light disappearing into the ceiling. Something caught his eye through a small window to his left. He moved over until he could see the dark street outside.

Now, in the hidden realm, he could see it—a faint glow of light, surrounding the building like a dome of protection! The prayers of this small group of people were protecting the entire building with some kind of power, straight from the hand of Elohim.

"You've got to see this, guys," Jonah said, bringing the others to the window too. They stood in wonder at the glow and the shelter it provided.

"That's all from people's prayers?" said Jeremiah, amazement filling his voice. "So cool!"

Eliza pointed at something across the street. "Look! One of the Fallen!"

Jonah, out of habit, began to pull an arrow from behind his shoulder and string it. He felt a hand squeeze his shoulder.

"Hold on, Jonah," said Camilla. "Watch this."

The fallen angel was standing on the outside of the prayer barrier, examining it closely. He spat at it in disgust, then turned back as if to say something. It became apparent that there were fallen ones lurking in the shadows just behind him. He'd been sent out to test the strength of the barrier, and he was being egged on by his companions.

The fallen angel took a few steps back, and then ran as fast as he could, headlong into the glowing barricade. For just a second, Jonah thought he had made it through. His body pressed into the wall, but then he rebounded. Almost as if the wall were a rubber band that had been stretched too thin, he bounced back suddenly, and fast. The other fallen angels stepped out of the way, protecting themselves, and he disintegrated into dust as he hit the wall of a neighboring building.

Jonah glanced back at the prayer circle. They didn't waver, didn't stop, and seemed as if they were unaware of what was happening outside.

Rupert, who had been watching the whole time with the look of a kid who'd just been punched in the stomach, spoke up. "What do you expect us to do? Pray here for the rest of our lives? Isn't there some kind of plan to get us out of here?"

As irritating as Rupert could be, Jonah had to admit that he had the same question.

"I am working with Marcus and Taryn on a plan, and will be in touch with my commander," said Camilla. "In the meantime, you are all under the command of Reverend Kareem. He will organize and direct the prayer barrier. Do whatever he asks of you."

She rushed out of the room, calling down the hallway for Marcus and Taryn. The kids all quickly exited the hidden realm.

"She didn't even answer the question," whined Rupert.

Kareem stood up quietly and looked toward the students, his eyes glistening as if he had shed tears while on his knees.

"Come on, guys, join us."

Jonah knelt beside Eliza and Jeremiah, extending the circle wider. Even Rupert and Frederick knelt. It would be hard to ignore the power of prayer after they had seen it in action.

The others had continued to pray, so involved that they seemed unaware of the presence of reinforcements. Jonah sat on his knees, trying to get comfortable. He fidgeted a little, which only made Jeremiah beside him fidget too. Finally, he accepted the fact that resting on his knees was not going to feel good and tried to focus on the words that were being said.

It took him a few minutes to catch up to the others. He heard words and phrases from the nuns like "supplication" and "hedge of protection" and other things that sounded high and lofty. But he also heard the simple, heartfelt words of his friend David, who was pleading with Elohim to protect them and naming each of the students out loud. This bolstered Jonah's confidence, and soon he found himself entering with his heart into the rhythm of prayer.

Although he was outside of the hidden realm and couldn't see the light emanating from the others or himself, when he joined in the prayer, he began to feel more and more connected. He focused on what the others were saying, and on allowing his heart and mind to reach out to Elohim. He found himself caught up in it, and he pictured the light being poured out of his heart, joining with the others, and sent toward the heavens.

TWENTY

THE WOMAN IN THE CHAIR

Even though Jonah found the prayer time to be exhilarating, his knees grew tired and achy, and after a little while, his mind began to wander. He swallowed hard, trying to push himself through the tiredness. It soon felt like swimming against a strong tide. He could tell Eliza, on his left, was also struggling. She kept rubbing her eyes mid-prayer and yawning.

Jeremiah was lying facedown on the floor. He could have easily been mistaken for a serious prayer warrior—someone lying facedown on the floor before Elohim, in full submission to His will—but his soft snores gave him away. Jonah reached over and shook him gently on the shoulder. Jeremiah raised his head, opening one sleepy eye.

"This isn't nap time, Jeremiah," Jonah muttered.

Looking around, Jonah noticed that a group of nuns who looked freshly rested had just walked through the door.

Kareem came over and tapped the three Stone kids on the shoulder to take a break. Apparently, they were praying in shifts now.

Jonah, Eliza, and Jeremiah walked out of the prayer room, stretching their legs. Kareem encouraged them to go back to their rooms and try to get some rest. Jonah knew he needed it, but he wasn't sure how he was supposed to sleep when a hundred fallen angels stood outside. *But we are safe*, he tried to tell himself. *The prayer shield is holding steady.*

They walked past a small side room, and Jonah noticed Camilla standing with Marcus and Taryn, huddling together. They were in a serious conference, and Jonah heard their voices growing heated. Jonah and Eliza stopped just past the door, craning their necks to listen as Marcus's voice rose above the two female angels.

"We don't need them, Camilla!" he said, the exasperation clear in his voice. "We need to simply attack them head-on. They will be no match for us." His finger tapped rapidly on the hilt of his sword.

Camilla smiled at the giant angel, her voice full of respect. "I don't doubt your skills, Marcus. But what would the children do if we should fall? Elohim has charged us with keeping them safe, so we must stay with them no matter how much we might want to fight." She turned toward a window, watching the fallen angels outside. A few of them saw the angel looking at them, and they began to gesture at her, calling out to her in some other language Jonah couldn't understand. But by their tone, it was clear that they were taunting her. This infuriated Marcus, and he pressed himself against the glass, ready to burst through and take them all on himself. Camilla extended her arm, placing it across the angel's chest, holding him back.

"It's what they want us to do, my friend," said Camilla. "Notice that they are not trying to penetrate the barrier anymore."

"It is too strong," offered Taryn. "They tried, but they cannot. There is power in the prayers of the humans and the quarterlings."

Camilla nodded. She watched them for another minute with peace-filled eyes, even as they continued to call out and beckon her to fight. "But there is something else. Something more . . . I haven't yet been able to discern it. But I believe that they are waiting."

Marcus turned toward her, fire still boiling in his eyes. "Waiting for what?"

Camilla continued to watch them. "I do not know," she answered quietly.

Taryn spoke, and Jonah could hear that even she, who was usually so even-keeled, was ruffled. "Have you spoken to our commanders? Are they sending reinforcements? Surely they recognize the need we have."

"Elohim will send us what we need when we need it," said Camilla. "You know as well as I do that the angelic forces are facing battles on multiple fronts, and our ranks are stretched very thin." She managed a weak smile. "Elohim gives us enough to accomplish His purpose. He always has, and He always will."

Both Marcus and Taryn lowered their heads, nodding in agreement.

Not wanting to get caught listening, Jonah and Eliza quickly collected Jeremiah, whose eyes were half-closed and who had propped himself against the wall. David had also been relieved of his prayer duties and caught up with them.

"We have a couple of hours to sleep," David said. "And there will be a lot to do once we get up." He placed his hand on Jeremiah's shoulder. "Come on, my young friend. We have to get you upstairs before you fall asleep on your feet."

Jonah let the two of them go on ahead while he walked a few steps behind with Eliza.

"The angels don't seem to have much of a plan, do they?" said Eliza. "You would think that Camilla Aldridge, the leader of the Angel School, who knows Michael himself on a personal basis, would at least have some kind of plan."

"Well, don't you sound a lot like Marcus?" he said, trying not to laugh. She only rolled her eyes at him.

"Well, maybe he has a point," she answered.

"Camilla said they were waiting," said Jonah. "Waiting for what?"

Eliza yawned, taking off her glasses to rub her eyes as they trudged up the steps behind David and Jeremiah. "While you figure that out, I'm going to go get a few hours of sleep before our next prayer shift."

She exited onto the third floor. Jonah, David, and Jeremiah headed to their rooms on the fourth level.

"You can stay with us," Jonah said to his brother. Normally, Jeremiah would have cheered loudly at the chance to stay with the big guys, but he just sleepily nodded his head and stumbled into the room.

Jonah and David checked the hallway up and down before they entered. They knew the prayer shield was glowing strong outside, but they agreed it was better to be safe than sorry when it came to fallen angels. Finally satisfied that none were around, they crawled into their beds.

Jeremiah was already asleep in Jonah's bed. Jonah carefully crawled in beside his brother and lay on his side facing the wall. Jeremiah pushed himself up against Jonah.

The warmth that the closeness brought sent Jonah, in spite of his worries, into a fitful sleep.

cʍɔ

Jonah stared down into a bowl of colored-marshmallow cereal, lifting a spoon to his mouth. Slowly his eyes focused in on the old wooden table, then the kitchen off to his right. He suddenly realized he was home, in Peacefield. But he was sitting at the breakfast table alone.

"Help me . . ."

Turning his head toward the voice, he saw a flicker in the den, the only light in the otherwise darkened room. It was coming from their old television set. A snowy image was coming to life.

He rose from the chair and moved closer to the source of the voice. Leaning down toward the television, he strained his eyes to see the blurry image on the screen.

A rusty, red door came into view, the edges outlined by faint light.

"Help me . . ."

The voice was coming from behind the door. As Jonah leaned even closer to the screen, the scene moved forward, toward the door and the voice. It was growing louder.

The red door slowly opened into a dark room. Shadowy figures were standing around the walls. He was unable to see their faces, but he felt the cold evil that was present there.

The voice was the loudest here. The scene on the television moved closer in, through the room, and Jonah saw that the voice belonged to a woman. She was sitting in the middle of the room, tied to a chair. Her hands were bound to the armrests, her feet were tied to the chair legs, and a piece of duct tape covered her mouth.

Her eyes were closed, but somehow Jonah knew that she was alive. And even though she couldn't move her mouth, the voice clearly came from her.

The sudden sense that Jonah knew this woman, or had at least seen her before, jolted through him like an electric current. He was only inches away from the screen when she looked up, opening her eyes.

A multicolored scarf covered her long dreadlocks, pulling them away from her face. Her gold earrings flashed in the light. Jonah took a deep breath.

It was the street preacher from Chinatown.

She beckoned him closer with a jerk of her head, as if she could see him through the television. He was entranced by the burning urgency in her eyes. She was trying to tell him something . . .

He blinked, and suddenly he was back in his bed. Another dream. And although the image faded away, the unsettling anxiety of it lingered.

She needed help. That much was obvious. But two more things became clear to him as he sat in the darkness, listening to his brother's heavy breaths beside him. She not only needed help—she needed *his* help. He had the unmistakable sense that he was the only one who could save her.

The second thing he felt was just as real, just as intense. He had to help her for his own sake. Somehow he understood that the survival of the quarterlings and everyone else he knew and loved depended on it.

PART III

THE PROPHET

"And he will go on before the Lord, in the spirit and power

of Elijah, to turn the hearts of the parents to their children

and the disobedient to the wisdom of the righteous—

to make ready a people prepared for the Lord."

Luke 1:17 TNIV

TWENTY-ONE

OUT INTO THE DARKNESS

Jonah quietly pulled his jeans and his sneakers back on, trying not to wake David and Jeremiah. He shuffled through his book bag until he found what he was looking for. Pulling the gleaming silver watch onto his wrist, he latched the metal clasp underneath. Studying it in the dark, he touched the button on the side. It lit up, a simple, elegant display of the time. It read 2:42 a.m. Nothing more, which brought a frown to his lips. He shrugged, unsure of the help he might get from the device. Tiptoeing to the door, he glanced back. Neither David nor his brother had moved. It was just as well. He didn't want to put them at risk. He was sure that wherever he ended up, it would be dangerous.

The hallway was quiet, as were the steps to the third level. He tried to walk as lightly as he could along the wooden floor. In spite of the occasional creak, he made it to Eliza's room without much noise.

He rapped lightly with his knuckle.

"Eliza!" he whispered as loudly as he dared, glancing back and forth down the hall.

He heard the sound of feet hopping from the bed onto the floor. The door swung open, and to his surprise, Eliza stood, dressed in jeans and a pink T-shirt, with a backpack on her shoulders.

"Hi," she said. "I thought that might be you."

Jonah looked down at her clothes. "Looks like you were expecting me."

She stepped forward, pulling the door shut and shrugging her shoulders. "It was weird. Something woke me up, just a few minutes ago. I had this overwhelming feeling that I needed to get myself ready. That tonight you and I were going to find the person with the voice."

Jonah squinted at her in the darkness. In the past year he had come to have a new level of respect for his little sister. No matter what happened, she always seemed to surprise him.

"That is weird," he said, "because I just had the most vivid dream I've ever had about it all." He quickly walked her through a description of the rooms he had seen in his vision, how hard it was to walk, and the encounter with the woman. "When I came to the last room, there were people around the edges, covered up in darkness. I don't know who they were, but they weren't good guys, let's put it that way. But the most important thing is that I finally found out who the voice belongs to."

Eliza leaned forward. "And . . . ?"

"The street preacher in Chinatown. It's her."

"The African woman?" she asked. "She saw us in the hidden realm, or at least we thought she did . . . Why do you think you've been having visions about her?"

Jonah answered her slowly. "I'm not really sure."

"She's more than just a preacher on a street corner. The visions, her seeing us in the hidden realm, her voice . . ." Eliza cocked her head and looked him in the eye. "Do you think she could be a prophet?"

"What I know right now is that she needs our help," he said as they began to walk down the hall. "Somehow, she has been . . . calling out to me or something. But there's something else, that I felt so strongly after my dream." He pulled the door open to the stairwell. "She's going to be able to help us too. And we're definitely in need of some help right about now."

"No kidding," she said as they bounded down the steps. "You know we need to talk to Camilla about this, right?"

He smiled back at her. "Where do you think we're headed right now?"

∽

"Absolutely not. You may not leave the protection of this convent."

Camilla's face had remained cloudy as Jonah shared with her his visions and dreams about the voice. Eliza told her about how she believed this woman was a prophet, and how she needed help and just might be able to help them too. The angel had listened with her arms crossed, but now stood looking out the window, seemingly taking an interest in the scene outside.

"The wall is still holding strong," she murmured, almost to herself. The fallen angels were loitering around, still waiting.

It crossed Jonah's mind that Camilla looked weary for the first time he could remember. Her face wrinkled in a way that reminded him of the human disguise he had seen her in so many times, an aging, elderly woman.

"Mrs. Aldridge?" Jonah said, to remind her that they were still here.

She snapped her head back toward them. "That's final. No more discussion about it."

"But—" Eliza began to protest.

Jonah grabbed her by her arm, knowing they couldn't say anything to change the angel's mind. "Come on, Eliza. You heard her."

He pulled her back to the doorway with him, and then turned toward Camilla again. "Is she a prophet, though? Is that right?"

Camilla nodded, still watching through the window, her voice soft and low. "Yes, dear. A prophet of Elohim."

He wanted to ask her more, but now clearly wasn't the right time.

"So that's it?" asked Eliza, glaring at him as they walked back down the hallway. "We're not going to do anything?"

Jonah was unable to keep a slight smile from crossing his lips. "I didn't say that, now, did I?"

They quietly walked toward the back of the convent. Marcus stood with his back to them, guarding the rear door. They were able to slip by him and down the short hall to the right. Jonah walked along the wall of the stained glass windows until he came to the one he wanted.

The image of Christ emerging from the tomb. He glanced at Eliza, putting his finger to his lips. Reaching up to the handle, he pushed. Silently, the window swung open. A rush of New York City air blew inside.

"I found this window earlier," he whispered. "I had no idea it would come in handy tonight. You go first, Eliza. I'll give you a boost."

He put his hands down low.

She sighed and rolled her eyes, but nodded, stepping on his hands. He pushed up, and seconds later she disappeared through the window. Jonah pulled himself up with his angel-strength, and with ease he fell through the window and out into the darkness.

TWENTY-TWO

ALLEYWAY BRAWL

They crouched down low and leaned back against the brick wall of the convent, blanketed in darkness.

"The only thing we have to figure out now," Jonah said, "is where we're going."

Jonah looked down at the large face of the silver watch on his wrist. It still read the current time, with beautifully scrolled hands, but nothing more.

"The MissionFinder 3000 that Marcus gave you last year," said Eliza. "It's not telling us anything?"

"It was a nice help to us back then," Jonah said, remembering how it had led them to New York in search of their mother. "But I can't seem to make it turn on." He shook it on his wrist, as if that would cause it to give him the exact location of the prophet. "How do you work this thing?"

"You know what Marcus said. These are usually given only to angels," said Eliza, twisting Jonah's arm so she could see it. "The mission comes down from his commander, and the coordinates are embedded in the watch."

"Well, we're sneaking out, genius," whispered Jonah, "so I don't think that's going to help us."

"But maybe we can get the coordinates from someone . . . higher up," offered Eliza, ignoring his comment. "Even higher than the angels." She raised her eyebrow at her brother.

Jonah understood what she meant. "It's worth a try."

Jonah bowed his head and began to pray quietly.

"Elohim, You are in charge of everything. You know what's happening outside of this place right now. If this is truly a mission of Yours that You are giving to me and Eliza, please show me right now where we are supposed to go and what we are supposed to do."

"And sorry for disobeying Camilla," Eliza threw in, peeking her eyes upward.

Jonah narrowed his eyes at her.

"Can't hurt." She shrugged.

He looked down at his watch again, pushing the side button one more time.

The watch began to transform in front of them. The scrolled hands disappeared, replaced by an orange glow. Jonah glanced up at Eliza, who was beaming as she looked at the watch face. Words appeared in an ancient-looking language that neither of them could read. It was in the angelic tongue, as he had discovered the last time he had used the watch. He pressed the button again, and the words changed to English:

Mission: Recover Prophet Abigail Honsou
Priority: Critical
Location: Manhattan Island, New York City
Proceed to Alphabet City.

"That's better," Jonah said.

Eliza's face lit up. "It worked!"

Jonah looked up from the watch. "Alphabet City?"

"I guess that's somewhere here in New York," suggested Eliza. "But the first thing we need to do is get out of this alleyway."

Jonah agreed. Looking out in front of them, he saw a narrow corridor that stretched for half a block. A crevice of light was visible at the end. He assumed that the opening, between two large buildings, would take them to a side street.

He didn't like it, but they didn't have a choice. They had to make it to the street ahead. *At least there aren't any fallen angels over here*, he thought. *That we can see, anyway.*

But they would have to run a gauntlet to get there, and just hope that they didn't find any trouble.

"You ready?" he asked Eliza. Jonah nodded.

After they entered the hidden realm, they saw that in front of them was a wall of pale white light. Looking up, Jonah noticed that it extended over the top of the back of the convent and down around it in every direction.

"The prayer barrier," he said.

They both knew what it meant to walk through it. One more step away from safety.

Eliza squeezed his arm and managed a smile. "We still go with Elohim no matter what. Remember what Dad always says? Even the darkness is like light to Him."

Somehow the words didn't comfort Jonah in that moment. He took a deep breath and stepped through the wall.

He felt a cool sensation as he passed through, but at least he didn't bounce off it and disintegrate like the fallen angel had. It felt the same on the other side, but passing through was a clear reminder that they were on their own.

They walked slowly down the alleyway. The glow of a distant streetlight cast a deep shade of yellow onto everything around them. Jonah could make out the outlines of metal fire escapes on each wall above them. Trash littered the street.

"It smells like the city dump in Peacefield," whispered Eliza.

"We would know, wouldn't we?" answered Jonah, thinking about their narrow escape from the Egyptians there a few days before.

He remained focused on the rectangle of light ahead that they were approaching. Another thirty steps and they would be out of the alleyway, and maybe he could breathe a little easier.

He couldn't shake the feeling, though, that eyes were watching them from above. He glanced up every couple of seconds but saw nothing.

You're just being paranoid, he thought to himself. *Stay focused on getting to the street, and we can figure out where to go from there.*

Just then, Eliza asked, "Does it feel like we're being watched?" Clearly he wasn't alone in his thoughts.

When he heard a scuttling sound, like rapid tapping against brick, Jonah knew it was more than his mind playing tricks on him. His head snapped upward, searching for what had made the noise. It sounded like something was crawling fast across the walls above them.

"What was that?" asked Eliza in a frantic whisper.

Jonah stood perfectly still, listening and watching. He couldn't see anything except the fire escapes above them.

They waited for at least a full minute, but it was deathly silent once again. Jonah caught Eliza's eyes and began to walk.

The scuttling above them began again, this time on both sides of the wall. Out of instinct, Jonah pulled out an arrow and strung it, holding it up above his head.

The glow from the white flame on the tip of the arrow illuminated the walls. Slowly, the creatures came into focus. Four fallen angels, crouched on the wall on all fours, clinging to the walls. Their black faces gleamed with intense hatred, and in an instant, they all leaped from their perches, unfurling their black wings and soaring directly downward as fast as they could.

Jonah fired his arrow, and it found its mark, tearing into the skull of one of the creatures. It screeched in agony, disintegrating, filling the air with a sheet of black snow.

Eliza had both of her arms outstretched, forming a strong shield of light around them both. The shield of faith was her specialty. The other three creatures saw it but didn't have time to turn away. They crashed down against it, their speed sending them careening off the shield and onto the pavement on either side.

One was now in front of them, and two more behind. They picked themselves up off the pavement angrily. Jonah had another arrow pulled, and he fired it before they could make another move. It ripped through one of the Fallen behind them.

The remaining two suddenly moved in unison, both rushing Jonah and Eliza at the same time. Jonah couldn't shoot both of them. Eliza's shield was holding strong, and he turned toward the one closest to her and fired another arrow over her shoulder.

It sailed through the shield of faith and found its mark. Quickly, Jonah turned back around, hand on his sword, ready to finish the last one. But the fallen angel was right in front of him now, just on the other side of the shield, no more than two feet from Jonah's nose.

Jonah fell backward. Stumbling into Eliza, he hit her legs, causing them to kick out from underneath her. Her hands dropped down out of instinct, to catch herself as she fell onto the hard pavement.

The shield disappeared. Nothing stood between them and the vicious fallen one, hovering above them just inches from their faces.

Jonah and Eliza began scurrying backward on the pavement, Jonah trying to get to a position where he could pull out his angel-blade, but the fallen one was too close. The stench coming from the creature almost made Jonah vomit.

The creature held a spear in his hand, and he raised it quickly, his eyes flashing brightly at the prospect of a kill. Or two.

Jonah raised his elbow over his face, waiting for the inevitable blow.

But instead of a piercing strike to his body, something soft fell against his face.

Black ash. Behind them, feet spread and still holding his bow, was David. Jeremiah stood beside him, fist-pumping the air. The fallen one had been blasted into a million pieces.

David dropped his arm, the bow disappearing. They could see his wide grin in the dark. "Got it! Not too bad, huh?"

So many questions ran through Jonah's mind that he didn't even know where to begin. Which was fine, because Eliza had no trouble figuring out what to say.

"Are you guys crazy?" she said, standing and dusting herself off. "You aren't supposed to be out here! Your job was to stay inside with the rest of the quarterlings. You're supposed to be asleep, for goodness' sake!"

Jeremiah shrugged off her questions with his usual smile. "I knew when Jonah left that something was up."

"So he woke me up," added David.

"You mean to tell me you were awake when I left?" questioned Jonah.

Jeremiah laughed. "I'm a pretty good sleep faker. Tricked you, didn't I?"

Jonah sighed loudly, but then chuckled.

"How'd you guys get past Marcus?" asked Eliza. "He was at the back door when we left. He's supposed to be guarding that post."

"Easy," Jeremiah said. "I just told him that there were fallen angels at the other end of the building. He took off down the hallway. And we followed you out that window."

"We saw you guys fighting those bad angels," David chimed in, "and we thought you could use some help."

Jonah brushed the black dust off his face and out of his hair. "Well, thanks for the help. But, Jeremiah, you know you're not supposed to lie, especially to a big angel like Marcus that could snap you in two."

Jeremiah looked up at him with his big, round eyes. "But I didn't lie to him, Jonah! I told him that fallen angels were at the other end of the building. And they are," he said, grinning at his brother and sister again. "I may not have told him that they're still on the outside."

Jonah sighed, looking back toward the convent. "Well, little brother, I hate to burst your bubble, but we're going somewhere that's too dangerous for you. We're going to have to take you back."

But as Jeremiah hung his head in disappointment, Jonah saw movement overhead. From where they were, they could see the dome of light that the prayer barrier made. Directly over the top of it, winged creatures swarmed. *They must have been there all along and we just didn't see them until now,* Jonah thought. They were probably searching for any cracks in the barrier, any weaknesses they could exploit.

Now, though, they apparently had seen them standing in the alleyway. They shot down the side of the building, positioning themselves between the convent and the quarterlings. There were at least eight of them, but more were careening over the building every second. Obviously, someone had sounded the warning, and the fallen angels were hungry for some action.

There was no choice. Jonah grabbed Jeremiah's hand and turned.

"Run!"

Jonah, Eliza, Jeremiah, and David took off down the alleyway. *If we can just make it to the street . . .* Jonah's thoughts focused on that one goal. If they could get there, then maybe they could find a way to lose them.

It was a big "if," though. Jonah looked over his shoulder as they ran. The Fallen were flapping their wings furiously, gaining on them with every step. Jonah bore down, and suddenly his feet felt light. He didn't have to look down—he knew that the sandals of speed that had helped him so many times in the past had momentarily taken the place of his basketball shoes.

He felt himself lurch forward.

"David," he yelled. "Feet!"

But his feet were already transforming too. Seeming to read Jonah's thoughts, he pulled Eliza into the crook of his arm and blazed ahead.

"On my back, Jeremiah!" Jonah yelled. He yanked his brother up, and Jeremiah latched his arms around Jonah's neck.

Jonah could barely control his speed while balancing his

brother, but he somehow made it to the end of the alley and onto the side road, right behind David carrying Eliza.

They turned right, two blurs running down the middle of the street. Jonah couldn't look back for fear of running into something. But Jeremiah was able to turn his head.

"They're back there, but we're way ahead of them now!"

Jonah bore down, beginning to move even faster, pulling even with David. He was determined to do whatever he needed to do to outrun the fallen angels. He was getting tired, though, and he knew he couldn't keep this up much longer.

He moved in front of David, making a quick left, another right, and one more left turn before he heard David's voice.

"Okay, Jonah! Okay!" he called out from behind. "I don't see them anymore. I think we lost them."

Jonah slowed down, dumping Jeremiah gently to the ground as he leaned over and held his knees. It felt like he had just run wind sprints in basketball tryouts at school.

"I wish I could run that fast," said Jeremiah, picking himself up off the ground. "That was so cool, Jonah! You guys should be on the track team this year."

Jonah and David just nodded, still sucking in air and unable to speak. Their sandaled feet were soon covered again with their normal shoes.

"Well, it looks like we're safe," said Eliza, inspecting the street they were on. "At least for now."

Jonah looked around. They were standing on the sidewalk of a tree-lined street. Cars were parked along the sides, most of them sleek, new sport utility vehicles and sedans. Along the sidewalk, sets of brick steps led to a series of well-kept buildings.

"This looks like a bunch of homes," Jonah said, glancing at the cars. "Nice ones."

"Well, that's great and everything," said Eliza, her voice full of sarcasm. "But we need to be looking for Alphabet City, right?"

"Alphabet City?" repeated David.

Jonah showed him the MissionFinder 3000. It still read the same. David whistled lowly at the silver watch.

Jonah took a few steps, searching the quiet street. How were they supposed to find this place? He knew a little about the city, but apparently not enough.

They needed to find someone who could take them where they needed to go.

A few blocks down, the residential street met with what appeared to be a larger boulevard. He saw a few cars pass by.

The silhouette of what looked like a taxicab was parked on the street corner, its red parking lights piercing the blanket of darkness on everything else.

"Come on, guys," Jonah said, beginning to take long strides with his lanky legs. "Who better to tell us how to get there than a New York City cabbie?"

TWENTY-THREE

A CABBIE NAMED SISERA

Jonah and David walked through the darkness toward the outline ahead. Eliza and Jeremiah were moving their legs twice as fast just to keep up.

"Hold on a sec, guys," called Eliza.

Jonah turned but didn't stop walking. "Why? I want to get there before he pulls away. You know how hard it would be to catch a cab at"—he looked at his watch—"three thirty in the morning?"

"Aren't you forgetting something?" asked Eliza. "That we're still in the hidden realm?"

Jonah stopped in his tracks. "Oh, you're right," he conceded, "it might be a good idea to jump back into the real world."

"Not the 'real world,'" Eliza corrected him. "I prefer 'physical world.' The hidden realm is just as real—no, it's more real—than anything else."

He held up his hands. "Okay, okay, Eliza. Let's just do this." He looked around. "And in the shadows over against that building, just in case anyone is watching."

They moved beside the cool brick side of a brownstone and bowed their heads.

If any human had been watching carefully, they would have seen four kids materialize out of nowhere onto the city street.

They hurried along, trying to move from shadow to shadow, knowing they could now be spotted by humans too, until they came up beside the taxi.

They heard music coming out of the open window of the cab. There were sounds of a fast rhythm and a twangy guitar, along with a high voice singing along to the music in a language Jonah was unfamiliar with. He thought the music sounded Middle Eastern.

Jeremiah started bobbing his head. "Nice tunes!"

Jonah motioned for him to stop as he and David approached the driver. He was sitting with his elbow resting on the car door, his eyes closed, nodding his head to the music, smiling, singing, and tapping his right hand on the steering wheel.

Jonah cleared his throat. "Excuse me?"

The cab driver must have not heard him, too wrapped up in his music.

Eliza had no patience for this. She moved forward and rapped her fist on the roof of the cab. "Excuse me, taxi driver?"

He jumped and turned to look at whoever was beating on his car.

"Take it easy on the car now, please!"

He leaned his head forward to take a look at the four kids standing on the sidewalk in front of him. He had tan skin and a dark mustache. A brimless cap covered his head.

The driver sized them up for a few seconds, wearing an easy smile. "You kids are out past your bedtime. Do your parents know where you are?"

Jonah looked at his companions, then back at the cab driver. He decided quickly that ignoring the question might be the best plan. "We're just trying to get somewhere and were hoping you could help us out."

The cabbie eyed him carefully. He must have decided not to press his question further. Instead, he smiled wider, displaying bright white teeth, except for two that were gold. "Well then, my name is Sisera. And I am your man! There is no finer cab driver in New York City than me. Hop in, hop in!"

At that, he jumped out of the car and opened the back door of the cab. Several gold chains dangled around his neck, with large jewels and golden images attached to each.

"Nice chains!" Jeremiah said, staring at his necklaces.

"You, my tall friend, should sit up front with me," the driver said to David.

Eliza cut her eyes toward Jonah, but he motioned her forward and into the taxi. The three of them slid across the backseat, Jeremiah in the middle, and Jonah slammed the door shut.

The cabbie adjusted his mirror so they could see his brown eyes. "Now then, where shall I take you tonight?"

"Alphabet City, please," Jonah answered. He added, "We're trying to get there as fast as we can."

"It is a big area," Sisera said. "Avenue A, B, C ...? East Fourteenth Street ... East Second Street ... somewhere in between?"

Jonah paused, looking at Eliza.

She leaned forward. "Fourteenth and A, please," she said, glancing at Jonah and shrugging her shoulders.

They saw his eyes in the rearview mirror. "If you say so. Fourteenth and A it is."

The cabbie eased onto the street in front of him. The music

was still on, and he actually leaned forward and turned it up, alternating between humming along with it and trying to talk to his passengers.

"Alphabet City," he said, watching them in the mirror. "That is a strange part of New York to take four kids such as yourselves. What brings you there?"

Eliza looked at Jonah and shook her head. Jonah knew what she was saying—there was no need to share anything about what they were doing with anyone.

"We, uh . . ." Jonah struggled to come up with a story that sounded believable. "Our aunt lives there. She gets up really early. We're visiting her today. And our friend David here . . . wants to meet her." But David looked lost in his own thoughts. Like he was trying to figure something out or remember something he'd forgotten.

Jonah wasn't sure his words sounded at all convincing. It wasn't like him to tell a flat-out lie to anyone, and it made him uncomfortable. But he tried to nod and look the driver right back in the eyes.

The cabbie's stare lingered on Jonah for a few seconds, and Jonah felt a bead of sweat pop out on his face. *He doesn't believe me.* But then again, why should he care what the driver believed? As long as he got them to where they were going . . .

"Your aunt, huh?" he said, flashing his gold teeth again with a grin. "Don't worry. I'll get you there as fast as possible."

He continued to hum as he drove, tapping his hand on the steering wheel.

They all seemed to loosen up after he had made a few turns.

"See, guys?" Jonah said, stretching his arm across the seat behind Jeremiah's head. "We'll be there in no time."

The cab began to pick up speed. He figured the cabbie was making good on his promise to get them there fast.

But then the car began to move even faster.

"Excuse me, sir?" a worried Eliza asked. "Aren't we moving a little too fast?"

Jonah's mind flashed back to a wild cab ride they had taken with their parents several years ago in New York City, but he didn't recall it being like this.

"What is the matter, young lady?" the cabbie said, his eyes suddenly wild in the mirror. "You don't trust me to get you where you need to go?" And then he began to laugh loudly and sing along with the strange music even louder.

He began making turns that threw them up against the sides of the cab. Right, then left, and right again. It started to feel like he was turning to jostle them around as much as possible. Jeremiah was in the middle, getting smashed and yelling loudly.

"You've got to slow down! Sisera, what are you doing?" Jonah called out.

David had been silent for most of the ride, but Jonah's words seemed to wake him from his thoughts. "Sisera!" he repeated.

But this only seemed to make the driver go faster still. They were now on a major thoroughfare, and he was weaving in and out of the other cars, easily going twice their speed or more. Jonah saw a string of four red lights ahead. Traffic was stopped at each one, but that didn't mean anything to their driver. He ran every single red light, narrowly avoiding crossing cars and buses each time.

They were all yelling now, bouncing around the cab and on top of each other. The cabbie continued singing and laughing.

They hit a large bump in the road, and Jonah felt his head hit the cab ceiling.

"Ow!" he said, holding his hand to his head. When the cab slammed to the ground again, they were all on the floorboard.

Out of instinct, Jonah prayed himself into the hidden realm.

He was not prepared for what he found there. The cab around them was gone. Instead of the black seats, they were sitting on a hard wooden bench. The entire roof of the vehicle had disappeared. Jonah's hand was bracing him on the cab door, but it was no longer a door. It was made of some kind of cold, grayish metal. It felt like iron.

In shock, he looked at the driver, who was still grinning and singing. His shirt had disappeared, exposing iron bands around his biceps and wrists. His hat morphed into an iron, dome-shaped helmet. He wasn't holding a steering wheel any longer. Instead, he held reins in his hands, thrashing them fiercely. Attached to those reins was a team of four gray horses. They were charging ahead at full speed.

One of the horses turned its head back. Smoke billowed out of its nostrils, and Jonah saw that its eyes were as red as fire.

They weren't really in a cab at all.

They were in a chariot.

It suddenly jerked to the left, and they were headed down a long, straight road. All of the lights were green now, at least. Sisera roared with a kind of twisted delight, and Jonah realized he must have found the road he was looking for.

The others must have seen that Jonah had disappeared into the hidden realm, and they quickly joined him. Jonah heard Eliza gasp as she realized that they were actually in an ancient vehicle.

"Sisera!" David cried out again. "I was trying to remember! The leader of the Canaanite army in the book of Judges!"

David reached for the reins but was swatted away, so hard that he slammed against the side of the chariot, dazed.

Jonah reached down to his side and drew his sword.

The Canaanite saw the glint of the angelblade reflecting a passing streetlight and swerved the chariot hard. Jonah flew across the laps of Jeremiah and Eliza again, his sword falling out of his grasp, clattering onto the floorboard. He scrambled down around Eliza's feet, trying to pick it up. But every time he got close to the blade, the chariot swerved in another direction, sending him and his sword in opposite directions.

"Jonah!" screamed Eliza. "Get it, quick! I think we're headed toward water!"

Jonah picked his head up from the floor and looked down the road. She was right. They were quickly coming to the end of this road. If they kept going straight, they were going to pass under a bridge. And then, on the other side, he could just make out the lights on a passing boat.

If this creature of the hidden realm had his way, they were all going to end up drowning.

David continued to try to fight Sisera but was getting nowhere. The strength of this driver was impressive.

Jonah narrowed his eyes, stretched down, and reached for the bouncing sword, but Sisera swerved yet again, and Jonah felt the hilt slide out from between his fingers.

"Come on, Jonah!" yelled an exasperated Eliza. Suddenly, she threw herself on the floorboard. A second later, she emerged with Jonah's angelblade in her grasp.

The horses were under the bridge now, heading straight for a dock that extended into the wide East River. It seemed as though they were traveling over a hundred miles an hour. In a few seconds, they would be hurled into the air.

Eliza was right behind the driver, Jonah's sword in her hand.

"The river, Eliza!" David shouted. And then he pointed toward Sisera. "Do it!"

There was no time to hand the sword to Jonah. There was no more time to think.

She pointed the blade at the driver's head and drove it into the temple of the Canaanite soldier. His scream pierced their ears, and he began to melt. In one last act of evil, he twisted his hands fiercely, even as they turned to liquid. He slapped the reins down as hard as he could, and the horses leaped. Sisera was nothing but a puddle. Eliza still held the sword, her mouth hanging open. But the chariot, having reached the dock now, had turned upward, flipping straight into the air.

Suddenly, Jonah, Eliza, Jeremiah, and David were ejected. Jonah spun upside down, unable to control his body. He could do nothing to brace himself for the impact of either the concrete of the dock or the cold, dark water below.

TWENTY-FOUR

ALPHABET CITY

Just as Jonah had begun to say what he was sure would be a short and final prayer, he noticed a flash of light. He landed on the dock, right beside Jeremiah and Eliza. But instead of his body cracking against the hard surface, it felt like he had landed on a thick gym mat.

He looked up to see that Eliza had surrounded them all in her shield, forming it into a bubble of light. It encased all three of them.

But David had been too far away. He wasn't in the shield with them.

The horses and the chariot had careened over the edge of the dock and down into the water below. Eliza dropped her arms, causing the shield to disappear, and they ran over to the edge. The water swirled and bubbled, but the chariot had sunk.

"What about David?" cried Jeremiah.

Jonah watched the water for another second but saw no signs of life. Pushing off his shoes, he poised on the edge of the dock.

"Jonah!" Eliza called out to him, but he didn't have time to talk with her. He jumped down into the water.

It was colder than he expected, and murky. He tried to open his eyes, but he could barely see six inches in front of his face. The only thing he could do was kick his feet as hard as he could and reach down into the dark, dirty water.

Just when he'd begun to wonder if he'd dived too far to make it back on one breath, he felt a hand brush against his fingertips. Grabbing it quickly, he pulled upward, swimming as hard as he could. He burst through the surface, his arm wrapped around the limp body of his friend.

"Jonah, over here!"

He looked up, and Eliza was waving to him, standing at the top of a ladder along the side of the dock. He swam toward it, and summoning his angelic strength, heaved David over his shoulder and climbed up the rungs, finally laying David flat on his back on the dock.

David lay motionless for a few seconds, Jonah, Eliza, and Jeremiah hovering over him. Jonah leaned down close and realized David wasn't breathing. He pushed down hard on his friend's chest to start CPR.

"Elohim," whispered Eliza. "Please save David. Wake him up!"

After Jonah's first few pushes, nothing happened. But then David began to sputter, turning his head to the side and spitting water out of his mouth.

"You're okay!" said Jeremiah, grabbing his arm and helping him up so that he rested on his elbows. Eliza patted him on the back a few more times, for good measure.

"Thanks," he said, shivering and coughing as he spat water

out of his mouth again. "Wow. I was unconscious, I think. It felt like a dream, and I was floating downward . . ."

Jonah smiled at him, putting a hand on his shoulder. "There'll be no floating downward for you as long as we're here."

David nodded, grateful. "Now Jonah Stone has saved my mother *and* me."

Jonah stood up, pulling his tall friend to his feet. "You can stop that right now, David," he said, brushing off the compliment. "You would have done the same thing for any of us."

"I can't believe we were in a chariot that whole time," said Jeremiah. "Who did you say that guy was?"

"Sisera was the name of the leader of the Canaanite army," said David, still shaking water out of his ears.

"From the book of Judges!" Eliza snapped her fingers. "When the Israelites had a female leader named Deborah."

"You remember how Sisera died?" asked David, his smile returning.

Eliza nodded. "A woman drove a tent stake through the side of his head."

"Whoa," Jonah said, thinking about how Eliza had just destroyed Sisera. "That's freaky."

"Well," said Eliza, looking a little creeped out but also rather proud of herself. "How about we not get into any more cabs, okay?" She directed her glare at Jonah.

"Why are you looking like that at me?" he said, returning her gaze with a fierce stare of his own. "How was I supposed to know that guy was really an ancient soldier who wanted to drive us into the East River?"

Eliza held her ground. "We just need to be more careful. We

could all be at the bottom of that river right now. You think Mom and Dad would be happy about that?"

"Can we agree to go find the prophet now? We're wasting our time here."

But where should they go? They all stood there, looking around for a minute, trying to get a bearing on where they were. Water was still dripping off Jonah and David. Jonah twisted his T-shirt in his hands, trying to squeeze out as much as he could, and he noticed David doing the same until they were both damp, but not dripping.

"Think we're any closer to Alphabet City than we were?" said Eliza, folding her arms to ward off the chill from the river wind.

As they walked off the dock and back to the street, it was clear that no one had an answer.

A man and woman holding hands and laughing with one another emerged from the sidewalk to their left.

"Let's ask them," said Jeremiah, and before they could protest, he exited the hidden realm and approached the couple.

They were too focused on each other to notice a small boy appearing out of nowhere right beside them.

"Jeremiah, wait!" Jonah said, right behind him. "It might not be safe!"

But his brother was out of the hidden realm and couldn't hear him. The only thing Jonah could do was keep a close watch on the streets around them.

"Keep your eyes open!" he called back to David and Eliza, who were already looking up and down the streets. So far, there was no sign of anything unusual.

"Excuse me," Jeremiah said. The couple didn't acknowledge him, walking right past like he wasn't there. "I said, excuse me!"

This time, the man turned around, raising his eyebrows at the kid standing there by himself.

"What are you doing out here, kid?" he said, glancing at his watch. "Kind of late, isn't it?"

The woman turned toward him too, but Jeremiah didn't seem bothered. He just stood with his hands in his pockets, smiling at the couple like it was the middle of day. *Maybe his personality is going to come in handy*, Jonah thought.

"We just need to find Alphabet City," he said. "And I thought maybe you could give me some directions."

The man looked past him and all around on the street. "Are you okay there, little buddy? 'Cause you said *we*."

Jeremiah stared at him for a couple of seconds, looking at him as seriously as he could. "I didn't say *we*. Are you crazy? It's just me out here."

The woman smirked at him. "Yeah, you did."

"No, I didn't, lady." Jeremiah wrinkled his brow and pointed his thumb over his shoulder. "Didn't you guys just come from that bar over there?"

The man and woman looked at each other and finally cracked up. "Good point, kid," he said.

The woman turned and leaned down, looking him in the eyes. "Are you sure you don't need help finding your parents?" she said, more concern than sarcasm now.

"How old do you think I am? Six?" Jonah said, forcing a chuckle. "My parents let me go out anytime I want. They're very persnickety."

The woman covered her mouth with her hand to stifle a laugh. "You mean *permissive*, right?"

"Yes, *permissive*," said Jonah. "What did I say?"

The guy just rolled his eyes and ignored the question. "Alphabet City, huh? You're in luck. We just came from there. It's pretty close. Why I'm giving directions to a little kid, I don't know..."

But he proceeded to point across the street at a large group of identical-looking brick buildings clustered together.

"The fastest way to get there from here is to walk south through Stuyvesant Town, those buildings right there," he said. "Just past them, you'll find the place you're looking for."

The young woman leaned over close to Jeremiah. "Are you sure you don't need some help? We could walk you over there or at least call someone." She was reaching into her pocket for her cell phone.

"No!" said Jeremiah, a little too forcefully. He cleared his throat. "I mean, no, thank you. I'm good. I can handle it from here."

He gave them a big smile and waited for them to leave. He even extended his right arm like a doorman, urging them on. "Bye now! Thank you!"

When they had giggled again and finally walked away, he reentered the hidden realm. Jonah, Eliza, and David were standing right behind him.

"You're crazy, brother. But good work," Jonah said. Jeremiah grinned at his brother's praise.

Again, they tried to stay in the shadows as much as they could, walking along in the hidden realm. Everything was both darker, and more alive, all at once. They passed the occasional group of people walking together but went out of their way to avoid them. Even at this hour, in the dead of night, there were people milling about. It was New York City, after all.

"I'm cold, Jonah," said Jeremiah, grabbing his hand.

They were walking through the Stuyvesant Town apartment buildings, which towered over them, creating another layer of darkness. Jonah felt more and more enclosed as they went along, but he tried to put on a brave face. "We'll find her and be out of here soon, guys. I think we're almost there."

He glanced down at his watch. It showed the time on the scrolled hands but nothing else. He pushed the button on the side but nothing happened.

"This thing is almost worthless," he said, disgusted. Eliza grabbed his wrist.

"We knew it would only take us so far," she said. "Remember last time? At least it told us Alphabet City. Apparently these things don't give specific locations."

Jonah nodded, remembering their last journey guided by the MissionFinder. "Once we were close, we had to trust Elohim to guide us."

He sighed. Just once, he wished he knew exactly where to go and what to do. A map would be nice, with a big fat X right on top of where the prophet was located. But he knew things usually didn't work that way. Not here. Not with Elohim. Elohim always seemed as interested in how they got somewhere as whether they actually did or not.

David's smile lit up the darkness enveloping them. "Even though I walk through the valley of the shadow of death, I will fear no evil, for You are with me."

"Maybe we should pray," said Eliza. "What do you think, Jonah?"

"Okay," Jonah said, stopping. Jeremiah reached out and grabbed the hands of David and Eliza, and they joined hands with Jonah. Jonah closed his eyes.

"Elohim, we're almost to Alphabet City. But we don't know where to go from there. We're trying to do what You want us to do. We left the convent, and almost got killed in a chariot ride that ended up in the East River. We know that, somehow, You are with us. You are here, like David said. So please show us what to do next. Show us where Your prophet is and help us get out of here as fast as we can."

Jonah peeked up, watching the fingers of white light extend through each one of them and upward, into the sky.

"Amen," he said. And the light slowly began to dissipate into the dark sky above.

The wind blew quietly between the buildings, and Jonah saw that they had almost made it through the apartment complex. Just a couple of streets over would be the section of Manhattan known as Alphabet City. He knew he was supposed to just trust, but new feelings of doubt began to push their way into his mind. How in the world were they supposed to locate one person in a place like New York City?

"I'm hungry," said Jeremiah as they walked along. "Do you guys have anything to eat?"

Jonah rolled his eyes. If there was one thing that was certain, it was that Jeremiah was always hungry. "Nobody has anything right now, Jeremiah. We didn't bring food."

He sighed. "But I'm starving."

"Well, you'll just have to wait until we get back!" Jonah said, a little more forcefully than he intended. "Besides, if you were that hungry, you could have stayed back at the convent, like you were supposed to."

"Okay, okay," said Eliza. "Let's not lose focus, boys. Jeremiah, as soon as we get back, we'll make you a big breakfast. How's that?"

"Pancakes?" he asked, a hint of a smile on his face.

Eliza grinned. "As many as you want. And lots of maple syrup."

The promise of a good breakfast seemed to satisfy him, at least for the moment.

"Now you're making me hungry," said David, rubbing his stomach.

"Does it seem odd to you that the fallen angels are just waiting outside the convent?" Jonah asked as they made their way across an empty street. Something had been strange about the way that the fallen ones were just standing around. Camilla had commented on it, but it hadn't really struck Jonah until now as they walked along in the darkness. "I've never seen any of them just wait before."

"What do you mean?" asked Eliza. "They couldn't get in. They were blocked by the prayer barrier. What else do you think they'd do but wait?"

Jonah shrugged his shoulders. "I don't know. I guess you're right. It just seemed strange to me. They don't strike me as the 'sit around and wait patiently' types. It makes me wonder what exactly they are waiting for."

Jeremiah, who'd been listening in, spoke up. "Maybe they're waiting for our parents to get there."

He said it in a matter-of-fact way, but it stopped the other three in their tracks.

"They are after us all," said Eliza quietly. "The nephilim too."

The thought unsettled Jonah, but he had to admit, it made perfect sense. Trap the quarterlings in the convent, knowing their parents would be alerted by the angels, and then wait for them to show up. It was a great plan if they wanted to get all of them in the same place at the same time.

"Maybe we should go back," said Eliza. "If they're just waiting to attack us all, we need to be there to help. I don't want to be wandering around in the dark out here, and then we come back and nothing's left." She swallowed.

David looked up at the sky, pondering this. "It is a point worth considering."

Jonah thought about this too, shoving his hands into his pockets. He walked back through his most recent dream in his head. "No," he finally said. "We are here now, and there's a reason for all of this."

Eliza looked at him, uncertainty filling her eyes. "You're sure about that?" she said, searching Jonah's eyes. "Because if we're not there and they get attacked . . ."

Jonah didn't know that he was sure of anything, but he had prayed and the MissionFinder 3000 had told him where to go, so he knew he had to trust Elohim; he nodded and steeled his face against the growing wind.

They emerged from the giant apartment buildings and onto a busy street.

"Fourteenth Street, like Sisera said," said Eliza, pointing to a street sign. "And there's Avenue B. Since the avenues are letters instead of numbers, this should be Alphabet City. Where to now?"

She looked at Jonah expectantly, waiting for an answer. Jeremiah and David stared at him too.

He waited for some kind of sign, any indication from Elohim of which direction would be best. But he didn't feel anything. Finally, he picked a direction, pointing straight ahead.

"Let's walk down Avenue B."

Jonah checked his watch. It was 5:01, and the sky was still dark. Streetlights illuminated the pavement and the sidewalks ahead. It was a wide street and more occupied than the neighborhood they had just walked through. Jonah was thankful for that. They passed an old man pushing a grocery cart, a loud group of college-age kids probably returning from a party, two teenage girls going who-knew-where, and a younger man in an overcoat, smoking a cigarette. Their presence made Jonah feel a little less scared, even though he knew they couldn't see or help the quarterlings if they ran into any more trouble.

Humans weren't the only ones they might see, though. Jonah was especially aware that they might come across other spiritual beings. It was only natural that they would spot fallen angels wandering around. They just couldn't let any fallen ones spot them and sound the alarm.

Eliza suddenly pushed Jonah, Jeremiah, and David against a glass storefront, into the shadows. She put her forefinger on her lips and pointed across the street.

Jonah looked and saw the outline of a dark creature walking on the opposite sidewalk in their direction. His wings cut an unmistakable figure under the street lamp—a fallen angel. Running his hands along the brick, glass, and doorways as he walked, Jonah could tell he was aimlessly loitering, not up to any good but not looking for anyone in particular.

He breathed a little easier. The fallen one had no idea they were here.

Jeremiah sucked a deep breath in, and Jonah could tell he was about to speak. He slapped his hand over his little brother's mouth.

The creature eventually passed, and Jonah finally dropped his hand.

"That was a close one," whispered Eliza. "We have to keep

our eyes open for more of the bad guys. They're probably every-where. The good news is that none of them know we've left the convent."

"Except the Canaanite cab driver," Jonah said, raising an eye-brow at her. Her face fell as she remembered that he was right.

"We destroyed him, though. You think he could . . . reappear and let his friends know that we're heading to Alphabet City?" Her voice sounded desperate, not wanting it to be true, but fear-ing she already knew the answer.

Jonah had no clue. The only thing they could do now was press forward.

TWENTY-FIVE

A New Weapon

B ut where to? They were finally on the edge of Alphabet City. Jonah's MissionFinder 3000 had stopped giving them any clues. His prayer hadn't seemed to get them anywhere, and they were walking down a street, an activity that felt more and more aimless the farther they went.

Jonah was about to give up hope when he heard a cry echo in his ears.

"Help . . ."

It was faint, so quiet that he almost didn't hear it.

He stopped in his tracks, cocking his head sideways. "Did you hear a voice?"

"No," said David, looking at Jonah curiously.

"I didn't hear anything," said Jeremiah. The blank look on Eliza's face said that she hadn't either.

"Is it *hers*?" she said.

He closed his eyes, straining to hear it again. Why was he the only one who could hear it?

"Help ... help me please ..."

It was the prophet! He was sure of it. But what direction was it coming from?

Jonah looked down the street. Avenue B continued as far as he could see. A cross street met it a few yards ahead.

He listened again. Her cry for help came to him one more time, very faintly, but yes, it was there. The voice sounded weak and tired. Yet suddenly he knew what direction it was coming from.

"That way," Jonah said, pointing left.

"Okay," said Eliza, glancing left and right. "Let's be careful crossing the street, though. It puts us right out in the open."

"Don't worry, Eliza," said Jeremiah with a confident smile. "David and Jonah can shoot arrows, remember?"

They moved across the street as quickly as they could, Jonah keeping his eyes peeled in every direction. As far as he could tell, they weren't being followed.

"Help me ..."

This time the voice seemed a little louder. This made Jonah more determined than ever, and his pace began to pick up.

"Come on!" he told his brother and sister, who were lagging behind the pace set by him and David. "Keep up. I think we're getting closer."

They walked two blocks, and he stopped to listen for the voice again. He closed his eyes, standing in the middle of the sidewalk, concentrating on shutting out all of the surrounding noise except for the prophet's cries.

Instead of the voice, though, he began to hear something else. It was a faint rumbling sound like thunder, rolling toward them.

Jonah glanced back at the others, wondering if it was like the voice, something only he could hear. By the look on their faces, though, he could tell they heard it too.

"What is that sound?" asked Jeremiah. "It sounds like a train or a stampede in Dad's old western movies. But nothing's there." He pointed his finger down the street and into the darkness ahead of them.

"It reminds me of the chariot we were just in," offered Eliza. "Except that it sounds like a hundred of them."

Whatever was causing the rumbling noise, Jonah realized that it was growing louder.

A cloud moved around the corner of the building three blocks down the street. It was dark, with sparkles of gold reflecting the streetlights.

Eliza pressed her glasses more closely to her eyes. "What is *that*?"

"It looks like a cloud of some sort," Jonah said, his eyes locked on the strange mist. "One that's moving our way fast."

David was studying the movement too. "I don't think that is a cloud."

It was close enough now that Jonah could see that David was right. It wasn't a cloud at all.

It was a swarm.

Jonah couldn't believe what he was seeing: a horde of creatures, flying toward them, the beating of their wings creating a thunderous roar. But they didn't look like insects. Instead, to

Jonah's horror, each one had a human-looking face, with a golden crown on its head, covering a shaggy mane of hair. They had torsos like a man's, covered with gray armor, but each had four brown, galloping legs. To top it all off, the creatures had tails that were swishing back and forth, raised up high, with a sharp point on the end.

"Weapons!" Jonah yelled, drawing his sword. David pulled an arrow off his back, while Eliza covered them all with her shield. Jonah pushed Jeremiah behind him.

They stood trembling as the creatures approached, now less than a block away. Jonah had seen his share of awful-looking fallen angels, but these brought ugly to a whole new level.

"They look like something straight out of the Bible!" Eliza shouted, hands raised above her head.

David focused his arrow on the lead creature. "I think they are! They look like Abaddon's locusts from the book of Revelation. You'll have to read about it later! Just watch out for their tails!"

As Jonah's sword was raised in front of him, glistening in the darkness, he glanced down at Jeremiah and considered the fact that maybe they should run, not fight. There were at least a hundred of these creatures, and he didn't see how they could defeat them all.

But David looked at him, seemingly reading his concern, and said in a loud voice, "1 John 4:4: 'You, dear children, are from God and have overcome them, because the one who is in you is greater than the one who is in the world.'"

Jonah realized it was too late to run anyway. The buzzing sound had grown almost unbearable. The locusts were upon them.

Jonah swung his blade at the first creature he saw, whose jaws were open, baring a mouthful of long, sharp teeth. The locust didn't try to bite him, though. Instead, it swung its tail around to reveal a pointed stinger, like a scorpion's. Jonah's sword sliced the locust in half, separating the tail from its body. With a roar of agony, it shattered into a thousand brittle pieces raining down onto the pavement.

David was firing arrows as fast as he could at the closest locusts to them. His arrows pierced one, then another. As Jonah was swinging his sword, he could hear the creatures wailing in pain before their bodies crystallized in midair and hit the pavement with a sound like crashing glass. Jonah quickly sheathed his sword and began to fire arrows along with David. Jeremiah huddled behind the three of them, unsure of what to do. He had no gifts yet to bring into the fight and could do nothing other than watch, occasionally calling out to the others when a locust began to get too close.

But the more arrows Jonah and David fired, the more locusts seemed to join in the battle around them. And to make matters worse, they were swinging their tails, more and more of them, jamming them into Eliza's shield of faith. As if they were trying to sting the shield. Although her shield was protecting them, it wasn't damaging their stingers at all.

Soon they were completely surrounded. And as hard as she was trying, it was clear that Eliza's shield was growing weaker. She was starting to wince with every blow from their sharp tails. "I don't know how long I can keep this up!"

Jonah looked around wildly as he continued to shoot, searching for any possible escape route. David was firing as quickly as he could, all the while calling on the name of Elohim.

One of the locusts screeched loudly, and the rest pulled back together. For a minute, Jonah thought it looked as though they might retreat, but it was just wishful thinking.

They charged the shield as one with their teeth bared and tails raised.

The blow of all their tails crashing into the shield together sent Eliza hurtling to the ground.

Her hands dropped. Her shield was gone.

Jonah didn't know what else to do. He pulled his sword out, yelled as loudly as he could, and began to swing wildly. He felt the blade slice through two of them at once, and he kept swinging.

It wasn't long before the side of one of the creature's tails slammed into him, so forcefully that he was knocked to the ground. His face hit the pavement, and he felt dizzy and sick to his stomach. He had landed beside Eliza, and David slammed into both of them. Apparently he had met a similar fate.

Jonah turned his groggy head upward just enough to see the blurry image of four massive locusts, hovering above them with their venomous tails swinging back and forth. They looked poised to finish the job.

Jonah didn't close his eyes, but just patiently watched as he awaited the final, fatal sting.

But then another shape moved forward, standing over the three on the ground.

Jeremiah hadn't been hit. He'd been behind them the whole time. Now Jonah watched in horror as he moved forward, within striking range of the awful beasts.

"Back off and leave us alone!" Jonah heard his brother's small voice cry out above the drone of the locusts' wings. Jeremiah's chin jutted out, defiantly daring the locusts to come closer.

Jeremiah's lost his mind. The thought rambled through Jonah's still-cloudy brain. *Why didn't I find some way to get him back inside the convent when I had the chance? Now we're all going to die, and it's all my fault.*

The locust hovering the closest roared and charged at Jeremiah. But he still stood.

"I'm not afraid of you!"

As Jonah looked on, sure he was going to watch his little brother die, something metallic appeared around Jeremiah's waist.

Before the beast could dig its tail into Jeremiah's chest, a loud boom sounded, and the creature was blasted backward, slamming into the others before shattering into a million shards on the ground.

Jeremiah was shaking, hands at his side, but still standing. Somehow, the blast had to come from him.

Three more locusts snarled at him, lowered their heads, and made a furious charge. Jeremiah looked momentarily uncertain, but gritted his teeth and stared them down again.

"Elohim is way more powerful than you are!"

Boom!

Another invisible sonic blast hit them, and they met the same fate as the first one, ending up in pieces on the ground.

The other locusts swarming around them paused, unsure whether to fight or retreat.

Before they could decide what to do, Jeremiah opened his mouth again.

"All of you need to go back to the pit of Abaddon, where you came from! We have Elohim on our side!"

Another blast, this one so intense that all of the locusts surrounding them shrieked in unison, right before they turned brittle and crashed into the ground.

There were others behind them who saw what happened and fled. They were all gone.

Jonah, Eliza, and David stood up, gawking at the seven-year-old in front of them.

"Jeremiah," Eliza finally said. "What is that you're wearing?"

He looked down and seemed just as surprised as she was to see, across his waist, a belt of silver. It was covered with intricate markings.

"Whoa," he said softly, running his fingers along the markings. "I . . . didn't want them to hurt you anymore. The words just came to me. What is this?"

Jonah moved in for a closer look.

"Unbelievable," he whispered, in awe of the gleaming piece of metal. "David, Eliza, what do you think?"

David studied it. "I think it's the belt of truth."

TWENTY-SIX

THE PROPHET ABIGAIL

H ow...what...?" Jonah sputtered as he eyed his little brother
with admiration.

"It's one of the gifts listed in Ephesians 6," Eliza said. "I guess
you had to figure it would pop up sometime. We just haven't had
a chance to cover the belt of truth in class yet. But I do remember
Taryn saying it is one of the more advanced giftings."

She smiled, resting her hand on Jeremiah's shoulder. "But
just like Dad says, Elohim is Elohim, right? He'll do whatever He
wants to do. And you, Jeremiah, got a pretty awesome gift."

"It seemed to activate when you spoke," David said.

Eliza nodded. "Not only when he spoke, but when he spoke
truth to the locusts."

"Totally cool," uttered Jonah, realizing David was right. Then
he laughed. "Makes sense. Jeremiah has been known to blurt out
the truth when it might be better not to!" Eliza laughed too.

David agreed. "You saved us, Jeremiah."

Jeremiah just grinned, looking down at his belt.

"But it's fading," Eliza said. "Look."

She was right. The belt was quickly losing its glow. They watched as it disappeared from sight.

"You'll have to begin to learn how to use it now," said Eliza. "Study it, practice with it, just like we do."

"Help me . . . hurry! Please!"

Jonah's attention was suddenly drawn to the voice again. Even louder than before. He ignored the others for a minute and strained to hear it.

Jonah reached down to his side and pulled his hand across his body. His glittering angelblade emerged again.

"Keep your eyes open and your arrows ready," he said to David. "Eliza, are you ready with your shield? Good. Jeremiah, see if you can get yourself ready to use the belt again if you need it. Now, let's go."

He continued to listen for the voice of the prophet, and as it grew louder and louder, he found his confidence—and his nerves—rising. At least he was sure now that he wasn't going crazy. But he had no idea what they would find. He kept going back to the dream, trying to figure out what the figures in the room with her looked like, who they were, how many of them there were, and what they were armed with. But he simply couldn't remember what he had seen.

They turned a corner and suddenly Jonah stopped. In front of them was a sign that read TEMPLE MISSIONARY CITY CHURCH. In pink neon.

"Temple . . . ," Jonah said to himself. "It's exactly how it looked in the vision!" He turned to the others. "We're close, guys."

Looking across the street, he noticed a large, metal-sided warehouse. One rusty red door faced them from across the avenue. "And that's the same door!" he said. "This has to be it."

Jonah stood, watching the warehouse for a minute, suddenly feeling uncertain about what to do next. Should they just walk through the front door?

David slapped him on the shoulder. "No time to get cold feet now. We're here. Let's go ahead."

Eliza fidgeted with her glasses. "Let's just be careful, okay?"

Jonah nodded, his eyes locked on the door. "Jeremiah, stay behind me the whole time, do you understand?" He knew he sounded like their parents right now, but he didn't care.

Jeremiah nodded solemnly. "Gotcha, Jonah."

"And be ready for anything," Jonah said. "My guess is there are fallen angels all over this place."

They hurried across the street. Two homeless men were leaning against the brick wall of the warehouse, asleep. Scanning to the right and left, they saw no signs of the Fallen.

Jonah placed his hand on the door handle and quietly reminded himself that their job was to rescue the street preacher and get her to safety with as little trouble as possible. The next steps were up to Elohim. He had no answers beyond that. Only the lingering feeling that she would be able, somehow, to help them.

The rusty metal door creaked open and they stepped inside.

Jonah held his sword out in front of him. Eliza's hands halfway lifted, ready to produce her shield of faith. David already had an arrow strung, aiming it into the darkness of the room they stepped in.

It took a few seconds for his eyes to adjust to the darkness, but pretty soon Jonah could tell that they were in a small room. The floor was covered with junk and garbage. Old, dusty furniture sat in random places, most of it turned upside down and broken.

Jeremiah stepped on a soda can, and the sound of crinkling aluminum made them all stop at once. Eliza glared at him and mouthed the words *BE CAREFUL!* Jonah waited for a full minute before he was satisfied that no one had heard them. They may not be so lucky the next time.

They finally reached another door at the far side of the room, cracked open just enough that faint gray light from the next room poured in, and Jonah leaned over until he could see through the opening. It was some kind of office area, or at least used to be. He could see a couple of desks along the wall, a few office chairs, and a bookshelf. But clearly none of it had been used for a long time.

Jeremiah leaned in.

"What do you see in—?"

"Shhh!" Jonah said, listening. He could have sworn he heard something. They all stood perfectly still, not making a sound.

There it was again. The sound of muffled voices.

"Did you guys hear that?" David whispered.

Eliza nodded. "Yeah. Sounds like at least a few people. I was kind of hoping we wouldn't see anyone except this prophet."

Jonah's forehead wrinkled. "Wishful thinking."

He pushed open the door slowly. It let out a loud creak, and he winced and stopped. His heart beat faster, wondering if they'd been heard. The murmur of voices continued uninterrupted. *Well, it's now or never*, thought Jonah. He pressed his hands against the metal surface of the door again, and as slowly and quietly as he could, pushed it open just enough for them to slip through.

Once they were all on the other side of the door, the voices grew louder. Jonah thought he heard three men, possibly four, talking loudly, occasionally laughing. He couldn't understand what they were saying, but it sounded like some of them were arguing, while another was laughing at them.

He motioned for Eliza, Jeremiah, and David to move over beside him. They were standing directly outside of the room with the voices now, and Jonah had a strong sense that this was where they would find the prophet.

The door to the room was slightly ajar, and he could now see a group of men sitting around a table. Four very large, muscular men were in the middle of an apparently very important card game. Each one had a Mohawk of bright red down the center of his scalp. They had on black T-shirts and jeans, and identical leather sandals that wrapped around their ankles. Four long spears were leaning against the wall in the corner of the room.

One of the men played his cards, smiling wickedly, and the other three threw down their hands in disgust.

"Come on, Frank!" one of the men began to shout, standing up and pointing a finger in his face. "You won again! You've got to be cheating!"

Jonah watched the guy named Frank reach up lazily, grab the muscular man's entire fist in his hand, and push him back down into his seat so hard that he toppled over backward. The other two laughed nervously.

"Come on, Frank," one of them said. "He was just kidding."

They were so busy arguing about their card game that they didn't notice the quarterlings watching them through the cracked door.

Jonah couldn't see what was on the other side of the room without opening the door wider. But if he did that, he was sure they would be spotted. He turned back to the others and took a few steps back from the door.

"There are four of them in there, playing cards together," he said.

"Humans?" asked David.

Jonah raised his eyebrow. "I don't know."

David and Eliza both peered in now, studying them closely.

"The hair, the sandals," muttered Eliza as she pulled her head back. "And the javelins. They remind anyone of anybody?"

"The bright red Mohawks . . . ," David said slowly. Then he snapped his fingers. "Like the crest on a Roman soldier's helmet!"

She nodded. "Roman soldiers."

"How do you know they're not just dudes with cool haircuts?" asked Jeremiah.

"They're not glowing," answered Jonah. "Since we're in the hidden realm, we'd at least be able to see a faint glow inside them. If they were human."

David whistled lowly. "Roman soldiers were fierce. They were some tough men. We need to be extra careful, guys."

"But somehow we need to get them out of that room so we can see if they're holding the prophet inside," Eliza answered.

"How do we do that without getting caught?" piped up Jeremiah.

"I have an idea, but you're going to have to trust me."

She moved to the other side of the room. Grinning at them, she picked up a stapler on a desk, cocked her arm back, and threw it across the room.

It smashed into the wall, and Jonah watched as the four Roman soldiers immediately jumped up from their card game.

"What was . . . ?" one hissed, and Frank barked out orders. "Somebody's in there. Go check it out! Get up! Now!"

Jonah stepped to the side of the door beside David, pushing Jeremiah back into a shadow against a row of shelves. One of the men shoved the door open, slamming it into the wall.

Eliza was already gone, back out of the other door and into the first room. Jonah heard another crash and knew that Eliza had thrown something else. At the sound of that, all three men, and even Frank, rushed into the room and through the next door, holding their javelins over their heads.

They pushed themselves even flatter against the wall. As the group disappeared from sight, Jonah knew that now was their chance.

"Come on!" he urged David and Jeremiah.

They rushed into the room. To the left was an African woman, her mouth covered in tape and her limbs tied to a chair so that her hands and feet were firmly fastened. The colorful dress and scarf she wore were covered in dirt and dust—it was just like in his dreams.

Jonah looked back over his shoulder at the door, then moved quickly toward her. It was definitely the street preacher who had seen him in the hidden realm in Chinatown.

Her eyes grew wide as she saw the three boys come toward her.

"Hey, are you all right?" Jonah asked, touching her on the shoulder gently. "We've got to get you out of here."

He pulled at the tape on her mouth, and her eyes squeezed shut at the pain of it ripping from her lips.

"So it's you?" she said when she recovered, looking at Jonah with a mix of amazement and curiosity. "I remember seeing you on the street. There was something different about you... Elohim pointed you out to me."

A bruise encircled her right eye, but even in this state, she smiled widely. "So you are the answer to my prayer? Well, Elohim always surprises. And this must be your little brother. You look just alike."

Jeremiah smiled at her and waved.

"Hello, ma'am," David said quietly.

She took David in. "And a fellow African for a hero as well?" She took his hand in hers and held it warmly.

There was so much Jonah wanted to ask her, so much he didn't understand. How could she see them? How had her voice reached him across space and time—and duct tape, for that matter? But none of that was important at the moment. "Our sister has led those guys out of here. We need to get you out of this place before they come back."

She was clearly weak and tired, but she nodded eagerly. Jonah used his angelblade to slice through the ropes with ease. The blade seemed to surprise her, but she made no comment as she pulled the bindings off her wrists and ankles, dropping them to the floor.

"Okay, we have to go, fast!" Jonah said, pulling her toward the door. All they needed was a couple of seconds and they'd be out of the warehouse.

That's when they heard the sound of loud footsteps approaching. Jonah frantically searched for another exit, but he couldn't find one. And they were coming through the door . . .

Two of the men walked back into the room.

"Hey!" one of them said to the prophet. "What are you doing? And who are you?"

The three boys stood beside the woman, facing the soldiers. One of them screamed a war cry and threw his javelin. Jonah swerved his head just in time to watch the spear jam into a wall and disappear.

"I told you guys," the prophet said as she rubbed her wrists, with a calmness that amazed Jonah, "Elohim was going to rescue me, and there was nothing you could do about it. I think it's about time we leave. What do you think, kids?"

Jonah caught David's eye, and in unison they pulled arrows off their backs, strung them, and released. Seeing teenagers shooting angelic arrows must have caught the soldiers off guard for a split second, and they were left with no time to react. The flaming tips found their mark.

For a moment, they sat squarely in their chests as the soldiers looked down at them. And then the Romans simply began to fall apart, as if they were made of crusty clay. An arm fell off, then a leg, another arm. Finally their heads hit the floor, and the rest of them collapsed in a heap.

"Ew, gross!" said Jeremiah.

Jonah looked at them in pieces on the ground. "Glad Eliza didn't have to see that."

Jeremiah grabbed the prophet's hand, and they moved quickly through the next room and back onto the street. Jonah searched back and forth along the street for Eliza.

There was no sign of her.

"Eliza!" he called out. "E! Where are you?"

Jeremiah did the same.

"I've got you now!" The voice echoed around the corner of the building. "Come here, you . . ."

Jonah ran around the corner of the building to find Eliza trapped against a chain-link fence at the end of a small alley. A thug with a red Mohawk was walking toward his catch.

Jonah summoned all of the angel strength he had and ran toward the man, slamming his shoulder directly into his back.

The impact sent Eliza's attacker through the air, landing against the fence right beside her. He crumpled to the ground, holding his head, dazed. The flash of Jonah's angelblade lit up the alley-way as it tore through the Roman soldier. They watched as he fell apart, just as the others had.

"Disgusting," said Eliza, backing away from the mess.

"Told you she wouldn't like that," said Jonah, smirking, as they rushed over to her.

"Are you okay, sis?" asked Jeremiah.

"Never better," she said, smiling. "Good plan, huh?"

They nodded together.

"You didn't forget about me, did you?"

The voice had come from behind them. They turned to find themselves face-to-face with the last soldier. Jonah saw the cold-ness of death in his eyes.

"Hi, Frank," he said. "You're not gonna fall apart like your friends, are you?"

The soldier smiled and tossed his javelin from one hand to the other, ready for a fight. "I don't think you'll find me as easy to manage, boy."

Jonah had his hand at his side, ready to unsheathe the angel-blade, but Jeremiah spoke up.

"Let me take care of this, guys."

Jeremiah stepped forward, and as he did, Jonah saw him bow his head slightly, and the silver belt of truth appeared again around his waist. Jonah was impressed that he was already learn-ing how to make it appear.

He moved toward the Mohawked Roman, staring him down as he walked.

The soldier chuckled. "This is who you're sending to fight me?"

But this didn't faze Jeremiah. He continued walking and raised his voice loud enough that everyone could hear.

"The truth is, because of Elohim, there is more power in a little guy like me than a thousand of you!"

The soldier couldn't help but begin to laugh. But in a split second, his laughter, and all of the rest of him, was erased by a loud crack, and an invisible wave that erupted from the belt hit him.

He froze, then toppled over, falling to pieces on the asphalt street.

TWENTY-SEVEN

A TROUBLING MESSAGE

Streaks of faint light were beginning to break across the sky. It would be daybreak soon. Jonah looked up and down the street, making sure they were alone.

"Hi, I'm Jonah," he said, extending his hand to the prophet. She smiled and took his hand in both of hers, squeezing it firmly as he said, "Nice to finally meet you. I've heard your voice in my head for a long time."

"Ah . . . that explains some of this," she replied. "My name is Abigail Honsou."

Eliza, Jeremiah, and David also introduced themselves, and she shook their hands warmly, thanking them for their daring rescue.

They began to walk back down the street, retracing the path they had taken to get to the warehouse. Jonah quickly told her their story, and then finally had a few minutes to ask her the question he'd been trying to figure out.

"So how did you talk to me?" he asked. "How did you know

to . . . get in touch . . . or whatever, with me? Do you have some special prophet powers or something?"

Abigail chuckled, eyeing him as they walked along. "Do you really think I was calling out to you?"

"What do you mean?" he said, confused by her question. "I heard you talking to me."

"Yes, but did you ever hear me call out your name?" she asked. "The first time I learned your name is Jonah was a few moments ago." Her eyes twinkled at him.

Now Jonah was really confused. "But how . . . Why did . . . ?" He couldn't complete his thoughts, much less his sentences.

Abigail placed a hand on his shoulder. "Jonah," she said, "do you believe in the power of prayer?"

"Sure," he said.

"And that Elohim answers every prayer that comes His way?"

"Yeah. I really do. I mean, I guess sometimes the answers aren't what we want, but, sure, I believe He answers them."

"Well Jonah," Abigail smiled, "thank you for being the answer to my prayer."

He shook his head in wonder, picturing Abigail tied up in her chair, tape over her mouth, calling out to Elohim for help. Of course she couldn't somehow mentally contact Jonah. But she had cried out to Elohim, and He had answered her.

And His answer came in the form of Jonah.

He wondered what would have happened if he had decided to just ignore the voice inside him telling him to act.

Jonah thought for a minute more. "I saw you."

She turned to him, intrigued by this. "What do you mean?"

"Like . . . a vision," he said, looking away. "A few times. In dreams."

"Has this happened to you before?" she asked, clearly curious.

"Yes," he answered. "Last year, when we were looking for my mother. She had been kidnapped by Abaddon's right-hand man."

"Hmm." She nodded thoughtfully but said nothing else.

"How long were you there?" asked Eliza, jumping into their conversation.

"Almost two days," Abigail said. Jonah could hear the weariness in her voice now. "I was on the street in Chinatown, preaching as I normally do. I have some . . ." She paused. "Special gifts. I am a prophet of Elohim, after all. But no one has ever bothered me before. Suddenly, though, I was taken, snatched right up off the street in the middle of a crowd of people. Not one of them did a thing to stop it."

"And then you were taken to the warehouse?" asked Eliza.

Abigail closed her eyes, nodding. "Yes. I must have passed out from the shock of it all. But when I woke up, I was tied to that chair just like you saw me in there."

"So you can see into the hidden realm?" Jonah said, unable to contain his curiosity any longer. "You saw us today, but you also saw me and Eliza that day on the street, didn't you? And you obviously saw your kidnappers."

Her eyes lit up. "Oh yes. Like I said, there are certain gifts that some prophets of Elohim have. That's one of mine."

Jonah wanted to ask her about her other gifts, but she suddenly stopped on the street corner. "Well, I've never seen that before."

The street ahead was empty, except for a few joggers, so Jonah bowed his head and popped into the hidden realm. Immediately, a tall funnel of whirling wind appeared in front of him. It stretched up into the clouds above, but it didn't make a sound. While he was staring at the funnel, Jonah sensed the others slide into the hidden realm beside him.

"Do you think it's . . . ," said Eliza.

"An Angelic Vortex," answered David. He looked at her. "What else could it be?"

"Maybe someone wants to talk to us," said Jeremiah. Jonah glanced at Eliza and David, and shrugged his shoulders.

They crossed the street, approaching the funnel slowly. Jeremiah grabbed Jonah's and Eliza's hands, and Eliza extended her other to David. He and Jonah clasped hands with Abigail. Then they all took one big step through the funnel wall.

After momentarily losing the ability to see anything and feeling a rush of wind, they found themselves standing in the center of the cyclone.

"Wow," said Abigail. "Impressive."

"Totally awesome!" agreed Jeremiah.

They were looking at an image that had formed on the inner wall. An angel had his back turned to them, clearly distracted by what was going on in the distance. He fired one arrow, and then another, ducking, and then crouching down behind a steel trash can. The chaos of battle was erupting around him.

Jonah knew who it was before he turned around.

"Henry!" he called out. "Henry! Can you hear us?"

Henry, their old guardian angel, turned around, clearly frazzled by the battle raging around him. "Jonah, Eliza, Jeremiah— is that you?" He craned his neck toward them as if it were hard to see. "It is! Excellent. I've been trying to reach you for some time now. We figured your approximate location, but without an angel with you, we had no way of direct communication. Glad you saw the funnel."

Eliza spoke up. "Henry, where are you? What is going on?"

Henry ducked down again, and behind him they could see angels and the Fallen fighting one another. There were also people who appeared to be human, but it was impossible to tell. He looked over his shoulder before he spoke again.

"As you can see," said Henry, somehow managing his typical smile, "we're under quite an attack by the Fallen. They've—" An explosion ripped through the background, and his lips continued to move, but they couldn't make out what he was saying. Other noises from the battle began to fill their ears. Apparently Henry's location was being overrun.

"Hope for reinforcements, but . . . Abaddon's forces are . . . prayer barrier didn't hold . . . quarterlings fell asleep . . ."

"Henry!" Jonah said. "We can't hear you very well."

But he kept right on trying to talk.

"I guess he can't hear us very well either," said Eliza, and then yelled, "Henry!"

All of the sound was gone now. The screen began to flicker in and out. They watched as Henry looked over his shoulder again, and either dove—or fell—to the ground. It was impossible to tell which.

Then the image was gone. The swirling cone suddenly stopped turning, and within seconds all was still.

"Henry looks like he's in trouble," said Jeremiah slowly. "We need to go help him."

"Worse than that," Eliza said, "it's obvious he was at the convent. Did you see the building in the background?"

Jonah grimaced. "It looked the same as the brick building across the street."

"Did you catch what he said? The prayer barrier didn't

hold," said David. "Did he say that some of the quarterlings fell asleep?"

"It sounded that way," answered Jonah. "The wall must have weakened."

"We need to get back now," Eliza said. "They need our help."

How else could they get back there, though, but walk as fast as they could? Jonah and David couldn't carry all of them with their sandals of speed.

They dug into the journey, but they were easily forty blocks away. Jonah figured it would take them about an hour to walk.

As they rounded the next street corner, though, a taxicab was idling. Three people emerged, and one of them reached in and handed the driver some money.

Jonah and his friends prayed themselves out of the hidden realm, and Eliza immediately started running toward the cab. "Cab!" Eliza shouted, waving her hand. "Taxi! Wait!"

"You want to ride in a taxi . . . again?" asked Jeremiah.

But she ignored him and ran up to the rolled-down window and grabbed it with both hands.

The old cab driver looked in his rearview mirror. "You got five. I can only take four."

Eliza motioned to her younger brother behind her back, and Jeremiah bowed his head and immediately disappeared into the hidden realm with a giggle. Eliza was not going to take no for an answer. She cocked her head to the side as she looked at the cabbie and countered innocently, "You must be mistaken. There are only four of us."

The cab driver rubbed his eyes, looked again, and sighed. "You got money?"

David nodded and got into the front seat of the cab, while

the other four crammed themselves into the back with invisible Jeremiah perched on Jonah's lap.

"Take us to the Convent of Saint John of the Empty Tomb, please. And if you could go as fast as possible—" Eliza instructed.

"Yeah, yeah," he said, holding up his hand. He stepped on the gas, lurching the taxi forward.

"You really didn't know we were coming?" Eliza asked Abigail. "So I can assume that you don't know where we're going right now either? Or what we're getting ourselves into?"

"I can see into the spiritual realm, as you have witnessed," the prophet answered. "I know things that other humans are unaware of—whether they ignore it or because I have been given an especially sensitive spirit." She paused, closing her eyes, as if she were trying to focus on something deep within her soul. When she looked up again, she peered deeply into Eliza's eyes. "Elohim's Spirit tells me that Abaddon is on the move. And I know that Elohim and the angels are organizing, responding, fighting, pushing back the darkness. If my prompting is correct, I believe we are going into the very center of the battle."

TWENTY-EIGHT

BATTLE AT THE CONVENT

Jonah, Eliza, and David did their best to fill Abigail in on the current battle. None of it seemed to surprise Abigail, but she took great interest in the details of their story.

Ten minutes later, with pink streaks lining the gray morning clouds, they turned onto Forty-Second Street. The convent was only a couple of blocks away.

"That's strange," said the grizzled cab driver, pointing ahead. "There's a garbage truck parked sideways, blocking the street."

Jonah leaned forward and saw the blue garbage truck blocking the road. It was impossible to see beyond it, let alone maneuver the cab past.

"Let's try the other side of the block," said the driver, and he whipped the cab to the right and took them around the next corner. They circled the block, arriving at the other side.

"This is crazy," he said. Another truck was there, parked in the same fashion.

He pulled over.

"Looks like you'll have to get out here," he said, turning to wait for his money.

"That's fine," Jonah said, digging into his pocket for the cab fare, and paid the driver. "Thanks for the ride."

"Ready?" said Eliza. Jonah and David nodded, and leaned over to pray.

They instantly disappeared from sight.

"What in the . . . ?" said the cabbie. "Where did . . . ?"

Abigail chuckled, winked at him, and stepped out of the taxi.

They walked around the garbage truck, and it was immediately apparent why the street had been blocked off. The convent had been surrounded—cut off from the outside world.

There was almost more going on than Jonah could take in at once. Angels were darting back and forth in the air, firing arrows and swinging angelblades at dark fallen ones. One group of angels flew directly in front of the convent, getting attacked from every side by a much larger force of the Fallen.

But something, or someone, was fighting them off at the door.

As Jonah moved forward, he finally saw who it was.

A group of people had positioned themselves outside the entrance. He could see Henry and Taryn firing arrows as fast as they could into the crowd. But there were others in the group too. And none of them were angels. Jonah blinked a couple of times. He couldn't believe it, but he saw what looked like . . .

"Mom! Dad!"

"Where?" said Jeremiah, who had been taking in the scene with his mouth wide-open. Jonah pointed toward the convent door.

Benjamin and Eleanor were standing with the group, all fighting off the advances of the Fallen.

"Hey, guys!" shouted Jeremiah as loudly as he could. "We're over here!" But they couldn't hear him.

Jonah suddenly recognized the others, apparently just as Eliza did.

"The other nephilim!" she said. "All of the quarterlings' parents—they're all here! Jeremiah was right. They used the convent as a trap, and now they're trying to get rid of all of us at once."

Eleanor was forming green balls of light, throwing them at the fallen angels. Some of the other nephilim were doing the same. Others were using their supernatural strength to push the enemies back. Cassandra, their guardian angel, was there beside Eleanor, firing arrows right and left. Somehow she had been recovered.

Benjamin stood with his back to the door and his head bowed, lips moving frantically. He was praying. And Jonah could see a rope of white light growing out from his father up into the heavens and around the people closest to him. He was praying for protection.

Abigail had taken a post on the side of the battle, beside one of the trees that lined the street. Kneeling, she held her hands out and began to pray as well.

Jonah, Eliza, Jeremiah, and David looked at each other, and then charged into the battle together.

Jonah raised his angelblade and swung hard at the first fallen angel he saw, blasting it into a cloud of black ash. David was firing arrows beside him. Quickly he picked off two of the Fallen who were closing in on the quarterlings' parents. Eliza expanded her shield as widely as she could to protect them. She also managed to produce the helmet of salvation on her head, for added protection.

Meanwhile, Jeremiah had produced the belt of truth again. Each time he spoke words of truth to a fallen angel, the creature shattered into pieces. It wasn't taking him long to get used to his new gift.

Two nasty fallen angels suddenly landed in front of Jonah, swords raised. He felt his hands grow sweaty, and he wiped them on his jeans to make sure he could still grip his sword. The bigger one swung at Jonah, and he barely got his sword up to block it in time. The blow sent sparks flying all around him. He pushed the creature backward, but the other one rained down a blow of his own. Jonah blocked it again, but it forced him to the ground.

He hit the back of his head on the asphalt, and felt a gash open up and begin to bleed. He blinked a couple of times, light-headed, and tried to refocus his eyes. The blurry outline of the two fallen angels came into focus, standing over him, displaying their wicked teeth as they grinned. They both raised their swords together, moving in for the kill.

A blur of light from Jonah's left, and the two toppled over and were sent sliding across the street. A hand grabbed him by his shoulder and pulled him up to his feet.

"Thought you looked like you needed a hand," said the blond boy, offering a smile.

"Frederick!" Jonah said, unable to hide the surprise on his face. "Thanks!"

They approached the fallen angels together, fighting back to back. It didn't take long for Jonah to pierce one with his sword, while Frederick blasted an arrow straight through the other.

The street was in total chaos. Jonah saw an angel down the street get hit with a red, flaming arrow and disintegrate instantly. Another one, who'd been battling in the air, fell to the ground with a great crash, exploding into white dust. Many were engaged in close combat along the street.

"Jeremiah!" he called out. "Eliza!"

But in the melee, he had lost sight of them.

He began to panic. A fallen angel charged him, but with his superstrength, Jonah grabbed him with his free hand and flung him against the wall. He slashed through his chest with the blade before the creature could move. But his eyes still searched for his brother and sister. Another flew at him from the air, but he raised his sword and thrust it into him too.

Some of the quarterlings were fighting on the street alongside the angels. He passed by David, who was positioned behind a car and firing arrows at the Fallen. Andre had somehow found a fallen angel's spear and was charging one of the creatures with it raised above his head. Julia was shielding Lania, who was expertly picking off as many of the Fallen as she could.

He saw a flash of white light and turned to see Eliza and Jeremiah standing with their parents. They had somehow managed to make it to the front of the convent with the other nephilim, and Eliza had created a powerful shield of faith, protecting them from the onslaught of arrows coming their way.

Jonah fought his way through the crowd, using his angelblade to cut a path through the Fallen until he made it to the nephilim and his family.

He could take in the whole scene on the street now. The fight raged on between the angels in front of him, the air still full. To his right, he noticed Kareem and the nuns. They had snuck along the building walls and joined Prophet Abigail in prayer together. Streaks of light emerged from them, up into the sky. He knew they were praying for their success, for the defeat of the Fallen.

But from what he saw, he wasn't sure that any of their praying or fighting was going to be enough.

And when his eyes were drawn toward a flash of movement above, he knew that he was right.

A man stood on the rooftop, watching. Even though the battle was approaching closer to Jonah, he couldn't take his eyes off the figure. Tall and thin, he could just make out part of his face in the growing morning light. He wasn't sure why, but it was a face that he recognized.

And then he placed it.

Roger Clamwater.

But even from this distance, Jonah could tell that there was something different about his appearance.

Maybe he's bringing reinforcements, Jonah thought, a shot of hope coursing through his veins. But that lasted only a second.

A creature came into view behind Roger, holding on to his shoulder as he hovered over his back. As Jonah watched, he motioned his arm forward. Who was he waving to?

"Oh no," Jonah whispered. Hundreds of fallen angels began to line the top of the building. Jonah looked back down at the scene in front of him and realized that this was only a small portion of all of the Fallen that were here. They were just the first wave, sent to wear them down.

Now the real attack was beginning.

TWENTY-NINE

PROPHET OF FIRE

They moved so fast that Jonah and the rest had little time to react. They were hopelessly outnumbered.

The Fallen made quick work of the angels in the air, relishing the moment every time an arrow pierced the winged beings. White dust began raining down around them, the only evidence now of the angels who had been protecting them from above.

Camilla, Marcus, and Taryn were still there, waiting on the ground. Henry, who had been positioned with the nephilim, hurried over to join his fellow angels. Samuel came rushing into the battle with his sword drawn.

Five angels, shimmering wings dulled by the dirt of battle, were all that was left.

Jonah's legs didn't want to move as he watched the scene unfold in front of him in slow motion.

A hundred fallen angels descended onto the five, who were standing with their backs to one another.

Jonah saw Henry's eyes flash angrily as he raised his sword, along with the others. Suddenly, the five were airborne together, soaring to meet the enemy head-on.

They met the Fallen with flashes of light and heat so intense it pushed Jonah and the others back against the wall of the convent. For a sliver of a moment, Jonah thought they might have a chance. But the force of the fallen angels was too great.

The impact of a hundred of the awful creatures sent the five angels straight into the ground.

And then beyond.

Their downward force blasted a cavern into the street, rubble exploding into the air. A thick cloud of dust blew up from the gaping hole. And then the street grew silent, except for a few of the quarterlings coughing from the dust.

The hole in the road was gaping, and Jonah, along with everyone else, had fixed his eyes on it, looking for any sign of life. Finally, he saw the outline of a large angel emerging from the dust cloud. Then four more, right behind it.

"Marcus!" cried Jeremiah, pointing to the silhouette. Jonah's heart leaped. Had they really survived the impact?

The first angel moved forward and into the light. When Jonah saw the sneer on his face, he knew.

He knew that all of the angels were gone.

The black, crusty creature stepped forward, followed by too many to count.

The first fallen angel said nothing but held up his hand to the sky, eyes moving back and forth to make sure all the quarterlings and nephilim were watching. Turning his hand over, white dust began to fall to the ground at his feet.

An audible gasp came from the parents and their children, who stood in the shadow of the convent, watching what was left of the angels blow along the gutter.

Jonah noticed movement again from above, something in the air, falling.

From the rooftop, two fallen angels had leaped and were floating down to the street. Between them they carried Roger Clamwater.

"Dad!" cried Rupert. Jonah turned to see the British quarterling, who had been standing behind him, push past.

Out of instinct, Jonah grabbed him by his arm.

"Let me go, you nitwit!" said Rupert. "That's my father there, don't you see?"

Jonah pulled him close. "Look closely, Rupert, and tell me what you really see."

"What are you talking about?" he said, turning and looking back at his father. The creature was still there, perched on his back, holding on so close it looked like a mere shadow.

"D-Dad?" Rupert said, pulling away from Jonah and stepping out onto the street, moving closer to his father. "What is this all about? You have one of those evil creatures on your back . . . *Where have you been?*"

The fallen one on Roger's back glared at the boy as he whispered furiously in Roger's ear. Suddenly, the nephilim's eyes found his son.

"Son! Come here," he beckoned, suddenly smiling.

"Don't do it, Rupert!" Jonah pleaded. "It's not really him! It's not your father!"

But Rupert couldn't—or didn't want to—hear Jonah. His

father held his arms open to his son. And when Rupert arrived for the hug he was expecting, Roger swung his arm across his son's body, backhanding him onto the pavement.

Stunned, Rupert scrambled backward, pulling off his broken glasses. "Dad? What are you doing? I—I don't understand."

Roger chuckled, a high-pitched laugh. "Sorry, son," he said coldly. "No time for pleasantries. Too much work left to be done."

Rupert stood and moved backward. "You're not my dad."

"Oh, that I am, my boy," he said, grinning wide. "I just like to think I've . . . improved."

Jonah's eyes darted back and forth, looking for any way out of this. They were trapped against the convent. He saw the nuns on their knees, continuing to pray, along with Abigail and Kareem. His eyes searched the skies for an angelic rescue.

But there was nothing. No one was coming. There was no deliverance in sight.

Roger, in the meantime, was clearly enjoying this moment. He paced back and forth in front of the nephilim and the quarterlings as he spoke.

"So nice to see my old friends, the nephilim, here today," he said. "You know, of course, why you are here, don't you? When you heard your precious, gifted children were in trouble, there was no way you could stay in hiding, was there?"

But suddenly the fallen angel holding on to Clamwater pushed the nephilim away, ripping himself off his back. Clamwater breathed in sharply, and then fell facedown on the asphalt, moaning in pain. The fallen angel stood facing the quarterlings and nephilim, his back to all of the other Fallen. It was as if he couldn't stand for someone else to speak for him any longer.

He wasn't the largest fallen angel Jonah had ever seen, but he strutted in front of them like he was their supreme ruler.

"I suppose I should introduce myself," he said with a twisted grin. "I am Dagon—the mastermind behind our little gathering here. Luring you here with your children was a stroke of genius, you have to admit. You just couldn't resist. Pathetic. And now, instead of trying to track you down all across the globe, you've come to us." He spoke with the slick assurance of a used car salesman. "Now Abaddon's forces can take care of you all at once."

Jonah began to tremble, fearing that what Dagon had said was right. Staying in touch with their parents had endangered them all. They could fight, but they were in a corner. Even with the combined powers of the nephilim and the quarterlings, there were too many fallen angels here.

"Maybe you should reconsider before it's too late for you."

The voice sailed across the street, echoing against the brick buildings, and caused everyone to turn their heads.

The prophet Abigail stood in the middle of the road, by herself. The nuns and Kareem continued to pray, just as fervently as ever.

Dagon seemed momentarily surprised she could see him. But then he smirked again. "I'm sorry. And you are?"

"I am Abigail Honsou. Preacher sent to the streets of this great city." She paused, her eyes glimmering. "And prophet of Elohim."

If this impressed Dagon, or worried him, he didn't show it. "Ah, yes. Aren't you the one we kidnapped? Don't you know that if I wanted to, I could order my associates here to kill you right now?"

"And if I wanted to," she countered, "I could ask Elohim, and He would destroy you all."

Dagon seemed amused, but she had gotten his attention.

"Obviously, prophet, you can see into the hidden realm. So you know that you are outnumbered no less than five hundred to one."

Abigail stepped forward with a confidence that amazed Jonah. "If that's true, then you won't be opposed to a test of sorts. Surely you believe that Abaddon is more powerful than Elohim, or you wouldn't be here."

Dagon snarled, the smile vanishing from his face. "This world belongs to Abaddon. *He is all-powerful.*" The fallen ones jeered loudly, voicing their approval. "But go away, woman. I don't have time for your tests."

"It sounds to me like you don't believe in that power, Dagon," she said. "Not enough to put it to the test, anyway. Maybe your Abaddon is not as strong as you pretend he is."

"Let's kill her, Dagon!" came a shout from one of the fallen horde. Others yelled their agreement. "Send her to her grave!"

The fallen angel held up his hand for them to be silent.

"Why shouldn't they see?" he finally said. "Why shouldn't they receive a full glimpse of the power of Abaddon, raining down upon them?"

Dagon turned to face the prophet, ignoring the nephilim and quarterlings for now. "Very well, *prophet,*" he sneered.

Abigail nodded.

"I propose that you call on the power of Abaddon," she said. "Call on him to bring his power down from the skies. If he's as powerful as you say he is, I'm sure this will be no problem for him. To prove I'm serious, I'll even offer myself up as a sacrifice."

"Abigail, no!" Eliza screamed. Abigail held up her hand to Eliza, ignoring her plea.

"Abaddon is from the pit of fire," she continued. "Call on him to rain his fire down and consume me. Let's see what he can do."

Dagon laughed again. "Have it your way."

He raised his hands up in the air, closing his eyes. At once, all of the fallen angels fell to their knees. Dagon murmured words that Jonah could not make out, but he knew that he was summoning Abaddon.

Jonah swallowed hard, wanting to be faithful, trying to will himself to trust. But inside he began to feel cold and dark, as if some weight were pulling him down.

Then, up above, a hooded figure suddenly appeared on the ledge of the building across the street.

"It's him," Jonah said. One by one, the quarterlings and nephilim looked up fearfully. The human parents, nuns, and Kareem just looked around, confused, unable to see what was happening.

The presence of the Evil One himself sent an invisible wave of fear and darkness over the edge of the building. As Jonah watched him, he felt the last drops of what hope he had left leak out. He was dry.

Dagon's voice had turned into a gravelly whisper.

"My Master, rain down your power now," he urged. "Bring all your power to bear on this insolent follower of Elohim. Do not let her challenge to you go unanswered, this mere human."

He continued calling on the power of Abaddon more and more urgently.

Jonah peeked up at the figure standing above them. He seemed to be basking in the calls of his followers. And then he raised both of his arms upward to the sky. Abaddon's hands began to glow a deep red. Jonah braced himself for what was coming.

But suddenly, the tendrils of white light coming from Abigail, Benjamin, Kareem, and the praying nuns shifted until they were pointed directly at Abaddon. They were joined with snakes of light that were falling from the sky, and they met in front of his glowing hands. Jonah sensed that Elohim was answering.

"Are you almost finished?" the prophet said to Dagon. "He's right there. Can't he hear you?"

Jonah strained to see Abaddon's face, but it was hidden underneath his hood. His arms remained outstretched. But the white light of the prayers seemed to be constricting him. His arms started to tremble and shake. Jonah could see his hands clawing, straining with anger to call his power down upon the prophet.

But nothing was happening.

Then Jonah saw Abaddon tilt his head upward into the sky and utter something toward the clouds above. And suddenly, the Evil One spun around, moved back from the ledge, and disappeared from sight.

Dagon, who had been egging on his master, stopped in midsentence. He stared at the place where Abaddon had disappeared and then looked toward the prophet. Jonah saw the confusion on his face slowly turn into the realization that he and his evil horde had been abandoned.

Suddenly, he pulled a fiery blade out and screamed in rage. Jonah couldn't tell if it was out of anger at them or at being left behind. The fallen troops behind him were on their feet now, raising their weapons too.

Their leader may have disappeared, but there were still enough of the Fallen to easily destroy the nephilim and quarterlings.

Jonah knew what he had to do. He moved over in front of Abigail, raising his sword in front of his face. Eliza quickly stepped over to join him, her shield blazing. And then, moving as one, the rest of the nephilim and quarterlings joined them, forming a wall of protection in front of the prophet. Jonah nodded at his parents, his brother and sister, and his friends, all of them standing together, united against the dark forces.

Their last, desperate stand would be here, protecting this prophet of Elohim together.

Dagon ordered the troops to charge, but the prophet remained focused. She bowed her head and raised her hands to the heavens.

The first wave of fallen angels flew toward them, but her voice carried above the battle.

"Elohim, Creator of all, You alone are all-powerful and in control of our world. God of Abraham, Isaac, and Israel, answer me today, answer me and my friends here. Make Your power visible today for the glory of Your name!"

Dagon and the horde of fallen angels were almost on top of them, both flying through the air and scuttling along the ground, their black wings hurtling them forward. All Jonah could hear as he braced himself for their charge was their bloodthirsty roar. The black wave, dotted with hate-filled yellow eyes, was about to crash on top of them.

His family and his friends were going to be overrun . . .

But not without a fight.

Jonah was ready to swing his angelblade when he saw the sky literally tear open and begin to roll up like a window shade that had been snapped. Behind the blue morning sky appeared an army that stretched as far as he could see in any direction. Soldiers on foot, wielding blades and spears, and men on horses with their hooves pawing at the air. Chariots, drawn by mighty steeds.

And all of them made out of fire.

There must have been thousands of them, all swirling flame,

causing the atmosphere to explode with red, yellow, and orange. The heavens were ablaze. Jonah realized that the rest of the quarterlings and nephilim were looking up at the sky now too. In unison, they let their weapons fall.

The Fallen were the only ones who didn't see the blazing sky above. Until it was too late. The army of fire fell down upon them in a furious blast of flame.

They landed all around Jonah, Abigail, and the rest, creating a wall of protection between them and the fallen angels, flames swirling around them.

The Fallen howled in rage, thrashing themselves around, trying to escape. But in their desperation they only slowed each other down. The soldiers swung their swords of fire, consuming the awful creatures. Some roared with fury and turned to fight, but they were no match for the army of fire and were quickly turned into piles of dust.

Within seconds, Dagon and the dark angels were no more.

Jonah had his arms raised in front of his eyes, guarding himself against the burning tongues of fire. When he lowered his hands as the battle grew quiet, he saw the army of fire departing as quickly as they had appeared, riding back up into the air. The blue morning sky folded back over them as the last of the chariots disappeared from view.

They were all catching their breath when Roger Clamwater stepped forward, having finally pulled himself up from where he'd been thrown by Dagon. Rupert approached him slowly. Roger looked miserable and ashamed. But his eyes were clear, and his back was empty.

Rupert embraced his father. They began to speak softly to each other.

"Look!" said Jeremiah, pointing upward. "More fire!"

Jonah's and Eliza's eyes turned up to the sky. It wasn't a soldier, but one solitary flame, descending slowly in beautiful shades of orange and pink. Abigail was looking up at it intently.

Suddenly, she turned toward Jonah and grabbed him by both shoulders, her face inches from his.

"Look at me, Jonah, and listen," she said, her commanding voice drawing his full attention. "Months ago, when I saw you on the street, I gave you two things—a word of encouragement and a warning. Elohim will use you for great things. Yes, I am sure of it. He already has."

Jonah looked down, humbled by her words. "I hope so."

She gave him a knowing nod and a smile, but her brow quickly furrowed. Glancing up at the sky, she continued, "But also, know this—you are in grave danger, Jonah Stone. Your very life, and the lives of your family, are at stake. Be very careful. Stay close to Elohim. Watch out for that devil. He knows who you are. But Elohim is greater. We have already won the ultimate battle."

"I will," Jonah said. "You can count on it."

Abigail beamed at him. "There's another thing too. Remember on the street, back in Chinatown, as I was speaking Elohim's word—do you remember how your chest began to glow brighter and brighter?"

"Yes," he said. His chest had felt almost like it would catch fire. "I do."

"Well," she said, "that's a sure sign of something—you're like me. A connection all of us share. Those of us who are prophets of Elohim."

Jonah's mouth dropped open.

"I'm . . . a prophet? Like you?" he said. "So the visions . . . the dreams I've had in the past . . ."

"Those visions and dreams you have can sometimes tell you what others struggle to see. Other times, they can tell you what is happening, even if you are not there to witness those things yourself . . . and sometimes maybe even what *could* happen, if certain things come to pass. There are even times when you will receive information from Elohim that not even the angels know. It is a wonderful, terrifying thing, this gift we share. But there is no mistake—*you are a prophet, Jonah Stone.*"

She eyed the flame descending toward her, growing closer and closer. Her voice sounded tired, but satisfied. "Your time has just begun. But now, mine is finished. Elohim has accomplished what He wanted through His servant. And I am ready. So very ready to go home to Him."

Tears formed in her eyes as Abigail smiled at Jonah, squeezed his shoulders tightly, and then walked over to the middle of the street, turning her eyes upward again. She raised her hands in the air and closed her eyes, a look of pure peace on her face.

The flame descended over her, hovered for a second, and then enveloped her entirely. The last Jonah saw of Abigail were her eyes, opening wide, with a look of both surprise—and delight. As if she had just seen something better than she'd ever imagined.

And then, like a breeze snuffs out a candle, she was gone.

THIRTY

MESSENGERS

B enjamin and Eleanor embraced their kids on the sidewalk. The five members of the Stone family stood huddled
together.

"Kids," Benjamin said, "when we heard that there was an
attack here, that they had discovered your location, we had to
come. I'm so glad you're okay."

"I'm glad you did," Eliza said, hugging her dad again. "But we
all could have been killed, you know."

"As long as the three of you are safe," said Eleanor, rubbing her
daughter's back, "your father and I would gladly pay any price."

It wasn't long before Jeremiah was telling a very dramatic
version of their rescue of the prophet, which kept his parents
spellbound and chuckling at the same time. Eventually the adults
gathered together with the nuns, Kareem, and the Clamwaters.
After talking for some time, they all knelt together in prayer.

Jonah was sitting on the sidewalk, watching the group with
David and Eliza. They were busy rehashing the battle, but Jonah

had been quiet, shaken by Abigail's words, and even more by her departure.

"Watch this, guys," David said, pulling Jonah out of his own thoughts. He nodded toward Roger and Rupert Clamwater, who were speaking with Benjamin. They nodded, and then knelt together in the middle of the street.

Another kid walked up and said something to Benjamin. Jonah watched as his father smiled kindly and spoke to him. Soon he was kneeling down with the others.

"It's Frederick," said Jonah in amazement.

As they prayed, Jonah and the others couldn't resist entering the hidden realm to see the beautiful white tendrils of light again, and this time they saw Roger's, Rupert's, and Frederick's bodies suddenly take on a glow, the same glow that all followers of Elohim have. In that instant, as they surrendered themselves to the loving Father, they moved into the Light.

"This is what this fight is all about, you know," said David. "It's what we are here for. This is the battle, right in front of us, being won."

"Remember the prophet Elijah?" asked Eliza.

Jonah nodded. "A little. Wasn't he the guy who—"

"Called Elohim's fire down from heaven." She smiled. "It burned up the altar that he'd built."

"And the prophets of the evil one were put to death," David added.

"Yep, and then the Bible says that he didn't just die like a normal person. He was taken up into heaven in a chariot made of fire." She raised her eyebrows at them, the connection to Abigail obvious.

"She was just like Elijah," Jonah murmured.

Jonah walked over to the place where the prophet had been standing only minutes before. There was something on the ground. He bent over, feeling the heat come off the asphalt, still hot from the flames. A piece of cloth lay there, all the colors of the rainbow represented in it.

"It's Abigail's scarf," he said, holding it up for Eliza to see. "All that's left of her."

"Just like Elijah's cloak," Eliza said. Jonah folded it up neatly and pushed it into his back pocket. He wanted to remember her.

Jonah, Eliza, and David slipped out of the hidden realm and walked over to join the other quarterlings, who were gathered together in front of the convent doors. Bridget and Lania were loudly congratulating everyone. Carlo was high-fiving every quarterling and nephilim he could, and Andre was walking around slapping his friends on the back. Ruth gave her brother a big, tearful hug. Even Hai Ling had joined in with the others and wore a smile on her face. Kareem and some of the nuns had come over and were speaking with them.

Julia stepped forward and hugged Jonah. He felt blood rush to his face, but he didn't push her away.

"I'm glad you're all right," she said, looking up into his eyes. As if suddenly realizing everyone was watching, she stepped back with the other quarterlings.

"Thanks," he said shyly. "You too."

Jonah greeted the others, and soon they were telling and retelling the stories of their battle with the Fallen. Everyone had fought hard. Frederick stood on the outside of the circle, staring quietly into the street.

Jonah excused himself from the others and walked toward him, clearing his throat.

"Hey, Frederick," he said. "Just wanted to say…thanks. Thanks again. You saved my life back there."

All of the arrogance was gone from Frederick's face. He nodded, shifting his feet, his hands stuffed deeply in his pockets.

"I figured you'd have had my back out there too," he finally said. He smiled, and they slapped hands together.

"And hey, I saw what happened," said Jonah. "There on the street. That was really cool. Congratulations."

Frederick looked at him squarely. "After what I've seen today, I'd be crazy not to give my life over to Elohim. I figured it was time to get on the right side of this battle."

Jonah nodded, and they walked over to congratulate the others.

But the thought of the fate of the angels dampened their celebration. Camilla, Marcus, Taryn, Samuel, and Henry were all gone. Crushed into white powder by the fallen angels. What would they do without their instructors and their protectors?

Then, right before their eyes, in the middle of the street, an angel stepped into view. Like she had moved through an invisible doorway. She had a starry haze around her, different from the warrior angels or the guardian angels Jonah was used to seeing. Her massive wings were spread wide. She wore no angelic armor and had no visible weaponry. Jonah wasn't sure what it was, but the air around her seemed to ripple, glittering with different colors as it shifted, picking up on the sunlight like a prism.

Four more of these angels stepped out of thin air right behind her.

The first angel stood in front of the quarterlings, who had stopped their conversations in midsentence, staring at her.

She smiled and bowed deeply. "I am Elizabeth, a messenger

angel sent by Gabriel for your service. We serve at the pleasure of our Lord Elohim. I have a message for you."

The students stood in front of the angels, hanging on every word from her lips.

"Well done, good and faithful servants," she declared. "You have served faithfully and withstood the attacks of the Evil One.

"But there is another message I have for you all," she continued. Her voice suddenly sounded grave. "You are not safe here for long. The Fallen know where you are, and they will regroup. You must come with us at once. Your instructors and protectors will join you."

Jonah, Eliza, and Jeremiah looked at one another. Jonah saw the same spark of hope in their eyes that he suddenly felt. *The angels had somehow survived. They couldn't die after all.*

Jonah raised his hand slowly. "Uh, excuse me."

The angel Elizabeth leveled her gaze on him. It was almost too much for him to take. "Yes, Jonah Stone?"

"Well, it seems like we only just got here. Do we really have to leave?"

She looked at him thoughtfully. "Only if you want to live."

Jonah sighed. Exhaustion was about to overwhelm him. But he couldn't deny the thrill that the words of the angel gave him, and the excitement he felt about the path Elohim had them on. He had no idea what was next. Right now, that didn't matter.

He stepped toward her, and Eliza and Jeremiah moved with him.

Wherever the road led, they were ready.

Acknowledgments

There are so many people to thank, who hold untouchable places in my heart and whose support makes some amazing things possible. Like life. And writing a novel.

To my kids, Bailey, Christopher, and Luke: simply put, you are the reason I write. You inspire me, make me laugh, keep me honest, encourage me, and help me dream bigger and better. You make me want to be a better dad. Your mom and I are so proud of you.

Mom and Dad: your relentless love for me has been overwhelming, tangible, and fuel for my sometimes-weary heart. I don't have to look far to see a picture of what commitment to a family looks like. Mom, you have shown me what selfless sacrifice to those you love is all about. Dad, your spiritual leadership has made a lifelong impact on me, as has your love of reading, stories, and books.

Bill and Martha: your tireless support of our family has been nothing short of amazing. You've cared for the kids countless times so that I could write. More importantly, you have shown us through your example that even in the middle of tragedy, God is still God, and that He is still good.

Amy and James, Jamie and Catherine, Brian and Dianne: you are the epitome of what family should be. Your enthusiasm and genuine excitement over these books have given me more strength than you probably know.

And to Dana, my second sister: there aren't enough words to express what you have meant to the kids and me this year. You *get it*, in a way no one else can, and for that I am profoundly grateful. You are irreplaceable.

To all of my family: your support during some of the darkest days of my life has given me hope, reminding me that the One who has begun a good work in us will be faithful to carry it on to completion, and that our trials, while real today, will one day be old stories to tell.

This book would never have happened without the wonderful people I've had the pleasure to work with at Thomas Nelson. Molly Hodgin is a brilliant, insightful, and creative editor. I'm grateful we've been on the same page with this series from day one. Thanks also to Micah Walker for keeping us on track and providing critical insight of your own. The entire Tommy Nelson team is second to none, and it was a privilege to partner with them on this book.

I also owe a special thank-you to author Robert Whitlow, who is both a friend and a mentor. Without your early encouragement for my writing, your wise advice, and your selfless generosity, these books would never have seen the light of day.

May God use this novel, and my life, for His purposes and glory here on earth.

Jerel Law
May 10, 2012

ABOUT THE AUTHOR

Jerel Law is a gifted communicator and pastor with eighteen years of full-time ministry experience. He holds a master of divinity degree from Gordon-Conwell Theological Seminary and began writing fiction as a way to encourage his children's faith to come alive. Law lives in North Carolina with his family. Learn more at www.jerellaw.com.

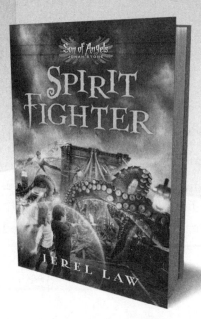

Travel back in time to London and solve mysteries with Sherlock Holmes's protégé!

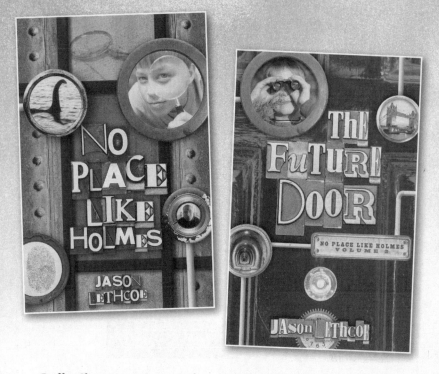

Griffin Sharpe notices everything, which makes him the perfect detective! And since he lives next door to Sherlock Holmes, mysteries always seem to find him. With Griffin's keen mind and strong faith, together with his Uncle Rupert's genius inventions, there is no case too tricky for the detectives of 221 Baker Street!

By Jason Lethcoe

www.tommynelson.com
www.jasonlethcoe.com/holmes

Check out all of the great books in the series!

No Place Like Holmes ❖ *The Future Door*

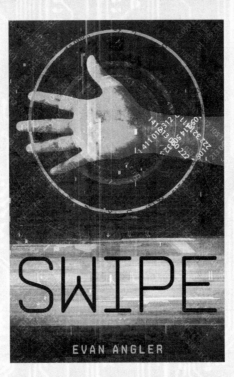